# SOME KIND OF BEAUTIFUL SIGNAL

# SOME KIND OF BEAUTIFUL SIGNAL

*Edited by Natasha Wimmer*
*and Jeffrey Yang*

TWO LINES WORLD WRITING IN TRANSLATION XVII

Endpaper: Ahmatjan Osman, "Oh, Night" from *Hussaty min al-lail.* Damascus: The Ministry of Culture, Syria, 2007. translated by Ahmatjan Osman and Jeffrey Yang.

Some Kind of Beautiful Signal
TWO LINES World Writing in Translation
no. 17

ISBN 978-1-931883-17-7

Cover photos and design by Ragina Johnson
Book design by Ragina Johnson, based on designs by Tag Savage

Printed in Canada by Friesens Corporation

Distributed by The University of Washington Press

TWO LINES is indexed in the MLA International Bibliography.

This project is supported in part by an award from the National Endowment for the Arts and a charitable contribution from Amazon.com.

# Contents

# Editors' Notes

There's an episode from one of the pieces in this anthology that I can't get out of my mind. In Henry Whittlesey's translation of an excerpt from Andrey Dmitriev's novel *Turn in the River*, Snetkov, a doctor at a mountain sanatorium in Russia, is sent a copy of Thomas Mann's *The Magic Mountain*. "You'll be stunned by the similarities," says the acquaintance who loans him the novel, but Snetkov proceeds to read it with a mixture of bemusement and irritation. From his pragmatic perspective, the book is a frivolous fantasia in which the characters enjoy every luxury but are simply sad testaments to the failings of pre-modern medicine.

For me, Snetkov's literal-minded, unapologetic rejection of Mann's novel perfectly encapsulates the stubbornness, directness, and independence of the prose collected here. Idiosyncratic but never contrived, the pieces ring with an unmistakable honesty. That honesty may take the form of deliciously unrelenting affectation (in Silvina Ocampo and Adolfo Bioy Casares's tale of a train trip to the seaside) or of delicate, clear-eyed observation (Mikhail Shishkin's "Verily He Is Risen," a tender account of the misadventures of a funeral party). It may shock, like Samanta Schweblin's surrealist fable of family dysfunction, or it may administer a jolt of humor, like Natalka Sniadanko's slapstick tale of tabloid crime and mail carrier perfidy in Ukraine.

Some kind of beautiful signal: that's what each of these stories sends us. When we read in translation, those signals may come from far away, but they are strong and insistent. Readers in this country have recently proved that they are willing to pick up on some foreign frequencies: the success of Roberto Bolaño's novels is a case in point. As one of Bolaño's translators, I've been in the fortunate position of witnessing how one writer can change global perceptions of the literature and culture of an entire region. Writers and translators—and readers—should remind themselves once again of the power of fiction in translation.

NATASHA WIMMER

The center of the poetry in this edition of TWO LINES is Uyghurstan (also called East Turkestan), itself the center of Asia, a region that has been politically called Xinjiang ("new territory") since its forced annexations by Russia and China in the nineteenth century; a land where ancient trade routes passed and western and eastern civilizations converged. The Uyghurs can trace their Tiek ancestors back more than two thousand years; their history and culture is rich and diverse, the people known to be hospitable and peaceful, as is evident in old Uyghur and Chinese texts. "The inhabitants live by trade and industry. They have very fine orchards and vineyards and flourishing estates. Cotton grows here in plenty, besides flax and hemp. The soil is fruitful and productive of all the means of life. From this country, many merchants go forth into the world," Marco Polo observed.

To the north, Uyghurstan borders Kazakhstan, Russia, and Mongolia; circling east is China; the south borders Tibet, India, and Pakistan; to the west are Afghanistan, Tajikistan, and Kyrgyzstan; and within its land, beneath its poetry and art, trades and songs, mountains and deserts, green steppes and grasslands, forests and strata-basins, are the coal, minerals, oil, and natural gas that are the primary cause, along with its central location, of the Uyghurs' modern oppression: the ongoing obliteration/underdevelopment of a people. What is happening? In this technologically dependent age, communications there (there being a country three and half times larger than California) have been completely shut down. Environmental pollution caused by industrial China has grown so severe that tuberculosis is the most common cause of death. The modern era of the Uyghurs has been marked by death sentences, executions, the burning of Uyghur books, mass foreign-population transfer, plus foreign government-military control of everything from agriculture to education to natural resources to media. It makes no difference that nearly every aspect of Uyghurstan, its people, thought, customs, languages, mix of religions, are as distinct from China's as traditional Hawaiian culture is from Anglo-America, or the culture of East Timor from Indonesia—some Uyghurs even have blue eyes and blond hair.

From this anthology's Uyghur-center the poetry radiates out through the pages, on its routes to China, Japan, Singapore, Malaysia, and Indonesia; to ancient and modern India, Chuvashia, Russia, and Iran; to Denmark, Germany, Oaxaca, Peru, Argentina, Brazil, and Haiti. My deep gratitude to all the contributors, especially to my new friend Dolkun Kamberi of Radio Free Asia—scholar, archaeologist, translator—for his vital help with the Uyghur Focus.

The anthropologist George Kubler has written, "Each poem in an anthology of related verse has its own systematic age, like each pot in a museum series, and each piece of sculptured stone." Poetry is an adventure, across time and distances. And how the world today seems to scream with poetry, its quietness, its stillness, its relentless regeneration of the word—the word as living spirit. *Morning star: like a signal / to stop.* Translation being thought's transformation, within the limited space of these pages, that our limits might be re-measured.

JEFFREY YANG

SOME KIND OF BEAUTIFUL SIGNAL

# Three Poems by Inger Christensen

Translated by Susanna Nied from Danish (Denmark)

When Inger Christensen died in 2009, European literature lost one of its most powerful voices. For over forty years she had combined virtuosity—including a genius for innovative poetic structures—with less tangible strengths: a clarity of vision and a generosity of spirit that emerged through her words, yet reached beyond words. Recreating her structures in translation is challenging. But the real challenge lies in the intangibles.

*Græs* (Grass, forthcoming in 2011), the second of Christensen's six poetry volumes, originally published in 1963, predates the complex mathematical/linguistic "systems" of her later work. Still, this collection of short free- and blank-verse poems builds to a final, 23-page prose poem in seven parts, with key phrases from the shorter poems recurring in the longer poem and again in Christensen's later volumes. This integrative continuity, one of her hallmarks, requires mindfulness in translation. Christensen and I began work on the *Græs* translation in the 1970s. Over the years, while translating her subsequent volumes, I revised *Græs* recursively.

These poems introduce themes that Christensen would pursue throughout her life: the primacy of nature; the exploration of boundaries between self and other; the crucial importance of human connection; and the role of language as both a means and an impediment to connection. Christensen's sociopolitical poetry is needle-sharp.

Her love poems are as wrenching as they are delicious. Yet, as the three poems here show, she maintained a belief in the human capacity for empathy.

In the poem "Contact," a personal relationship expands toward social consciousness. The speaker struggles to relate to one other person, a "you" with an "alien hand." What is alien is also frightening; the effort to achieve true contact, beyond language, is daunting. One "you" becomes many, "who all have alien hands / that are slowly moved and exchanged / the weak the strong..." The last lines, not quite mirroring the first, create a circle as fragile as contact itself.

In "Whispering Grassfeet," boundaries blur as self and nature merge. Two people walk a forest path; the path's own grassy feet walk through them. Their fingers touch, become branches. The two become the urgency of birds in summer, drilling at fir-cone hearts. Words, too, merge (*grassfeet, summer-greedy*); alliteration bridges lines; irregular dactyls hint at a heartbeat. Christensen's shapeshifting incantation is worthy of the *Elder Edda*—

or a Zen master.

In "Otherness Touched," syntax dissolves as boundaries dissolve. Verbs are scarce. There is an interlude of "silence," a spare and exquisite eroticism: "flecks of grass on sated skin," a "changing to and from place," "your voice" and "your body" on the forest floor. And still, there is separateness. It never really disappears. But for a moment, "otherness at last" is "touched."

Inger Christensen's works have been translated into more than thirty languages. She won many international literary awards. The most telling tributes, however, may be those left by the reading public on a memorial website after her death. There, reader after reader wrote simply, "Tak, Inger." Thank you, Inger.

Original text: Inger Christensen, *Græs: Digte af Inger Christensen.* Copenhagen: Gyldendal, 1963, 1983.

# Kontakt

Tegne en spinkel cirkel
i luft eller vand
lægge en finger på munden
og afdæmpe troen
lægge en hånd på hjertet
svare dig ærligt:
ingenting svare
ingenting ønske
forsvare din fremmede hånd
med åbne arme
forsvare de svage
med tillid

svare de stærke
med tillid
de stærke og svæge
som alle har fremmede hænder
som alle har fremmede hænder
der langsomt bevæges og byttes
de svage de stærke
svare dig ærligt
tegne en cirkel
i luft eller vand

# Contact

To sketch a spindly circle
in water or air
put a finger to my lips
and quiet the belief
put a hand to my heart
answer you honestly:
to answer nothing
wish nothing
defend your alien hand
with open arms
defend the weak
with faith

answer the strong
with faith
the strong and the weak
who all have alien hands
who all have alien hands
that are slowly moved and exchanged
the weak the strong
to answer you honestly
sketch a circle
in water or air

# Hviskende græsfødder

Hviskende græsfødder
lister sig gennem os,
granfingre rører hinanden
når stierne mødes,
sejg svedende harpiks
klæber os sammen,
sommerbegærlige spætter
hakker i hårdføre
frøgemmehjerter.

# Whispering Grassfeet

Whispering grassfeet
steal through us
fir-fingers touch one another
where the paths meet
thick dripping resin
glues us together
summer-greedy woodpeckers
hammer at hardy
seed-hiding hearts

# Andet berørt

Andet berørt. Endnu med pletter af græs
    på den mættede hud som i stilhed

Endnu med blade på hænder og fødder
    sted som til sidst

Andet til sidst. Som skiftende
    til og fra blivende sted
    er hér

Andet som husker din stemme
    i gråbrun svamp

Søvn som i prikkende nåle husker
    din krop en solplet

Endnu med urtågens farve

Endnu med adskilt

Adskilt som fører dig adskilt

Endnu med græs efter græs

Ind i et andet til sidst

som berørt

# Otherness Touched

Otherness touched. Still with flecks
 of grass on sated skin as in silence

Still with leaves on hands and
 feet place as at last

Otherness at last. That changing
 to and from lasting place
 is here

Otherness that remembers your voice
 in gray-brown forest fungi

Sleep that in prickling needles
 remembers your body
 a sunfleck

Still with primal fog colors

Still with separate

Separate that leads you separate

Still with grass after grass

Into an otherness at last

as touched

# Madame Bovary

Gustave Flaubert | Translated by Lydia Davis from French (France)

"Yesterday evening, I started my novel. Now I begin to see stylistic difficulties that horrify me. To be simple is no small matter." This is what Flaubert wrote to his friend, lover, and fellow writer Louise Colet on the evening of September 20, 1851, and the novel he was referring to was *Madame Bovary*. He was just under 30 years old.

Flaubert spent about four and a half years writing the novel, staying closeted with his work for months at a time, only periodically taking the train to Paris for some days of city life and sociability with friends, though he did not always stop working when he was there.

He finished it sometime in March of 1856; it was then accepted for publication by his longtime friend Maxime Du Camp, one of the editors of the *Revue de Paris*, and it was published serially in that journal in six installments from October 1 to December 15.

Although certain scenes had been cut from this version as a precaution—which perhaps had the opposite effect of arousing suspicions—the government brought charges against it for being a danger to morality and religion. The trial took place January 29, 1857, and lasted one day; Flaubert and the magazine were acquitted a week later.

The very approach that made the novel vulnerable to

prosecution by the Second Empire government was what made it so radical for fiction of its day—it depicted the lives of its characters objectively, without idealizing, without romanticizing, and without intent to instruct or to draw a moral lesson. The novel, soon to be labeled "realist" by his contemporaries, though Flaubert resisted the label, as he resisted belonging to any literary "school," is now viewed as the first masterpiece of realist fiction. Yet its radical nature is paradoxically difficult for us to see: its approach is familiar to us for the very reason that *Madame Bovary* permanently changed the way novels were written thereafter.

...The story contains no sermon to point out its moral; it has no "good" moral exemplar to offer in contrast to the "bad" woman that Emma is. The author does not condemn her for her behavior but, rather, may even have some sympathy for her, nor does he pass judgment on any of the other characters. The story is uncompromising: the heroine commits adultery and then suicide; her good husband dies, too; her innocent child is fated to have a hard life; the evil moneylender who has been the instrument of Emma's downfall prospers; the conniving, hypocritical, and disloyal "friend," Homais, is rewarded with a coveted medal.

Flaubert's aim was to write the novel "objectively," leaving the author out of it. Although *Madame Bovary* is filled with political and social detail reflecting Flaubert's very strong views (Zola describes how Flaubert could not tolerate being contradicted in an argument), his technique is to present the material without comment, though occasionally comment does slip in. To report the facts objectively, to give a painstaking objective description—of a ridiculous object, for instance—should be comment enough.*

✣

My approach to translating *Madame Bovary* was the same as my approach to translating Marcel Proust's *Swann's Way* a few years ago, and, in fact, almost every previous translation I've done: to follow the original very closely, though of course not slavishly. I tried to depart as little as possible from the way the sentences unfolded in the original, and to add and subtract nothing, attempting to use equivalent sorts of words and reproduce the same level of diction that Flaubert employed, and all the while, of course, doing my best to compose a piece of writing that was strong, natural, and effective in English. I didn't ask myself in advance: "How will I convey Flaubert's irony at this point?" for example, but trusted that if I adhered closely to what he wrote, the irony would come through.

It is surprising, really, how many translators do not take this approach, which is either easier or harder, depending on one's temperament I suppose, than taking the opposite approach—recasting the sentence completely, changing at will the order of elements, type of vocabulary, level of diction, adding a phrase here and there, omitting something awkward. As I consulted the eleven previous translations of *Madame Bovary* into English that I acquired in the course of doing this work, I found what should have been the obvious answer to a long-standing question of mine: When I first read *Madame Bovary* decades ago—in translation—I wondered, naively, why so much fuss had been made about Flaubert's famous style, since the style of the novel did not seem either anything special or even particularly effective. It did not occur to me that what I was reading was not his style but the translator's, and that his style had simply not survived translation into English!

During my work on the second draft of this translation, as I examined the other translations I had at hand, I saw, amid the wide range of approaches, that the better writers tended to depart needlessly far from the original—rearranging or recombining sentences, amplifying freely, adding metaphors, phrases, even whole sentences, and inevitably thereby changing the tone, style, and in fact the very substance of what Flaubert had written—while the more literal translators were not especially gifted writers. And so I have tried to supply what I feel was missing—a translation that is faithful and also well written. But of course any translation is always a compromise, and the experience of reading a translation can never be quite the same as that of reading the original.

* Pages 12-14, adapted from Lydia Davis's introduction to *Madame Bovary*, Viking Penguin, 2010.

# Madame Bovary

2

Une nuit, vers onze heures, ils furent réveillés par le bruit d'un cheval qui s'arrêta juste à la porte. La bonne ouvrit la lucarne du grenier et parlementa quelque temps avec un homme resté en bas, dans la rue. Il venait chercher le médecin; il avait une lettre. *Nastasie* descendit les marches en grelottant, et alla ouvrir la serrure et les verrous, l'un après l'autre. L'homme laissa son cheval, et, suivant la bonne, entra tout à coup derrière elle. Il tira de dedans son bonnet de laine à houppes grises, une lettre enveloppée dans un chiffon, et la présenta délicatement à Charles, qui s'accouda sur l'oreiller pour la lire. Nastasie, près du lit, tenait la lumière. Madame, par pudeur, restait tournée vers la ruelle et montrait le dos.

Cette lettre, cachetée d'un petit cachet de cire bleue, suppliait M. Bovary de se rendre immédiatement à la ferme des Bertaux, pour remettre une jambe cassée. Or il y a, de Tostes aux Bertaux, six bonnes lieues de traverse, en passant par Longueville et Saint-Victor. La nuit était noire. Madame Bovary jeune redoutait les accidents pour son mari. Donc il fut décidé que le valet d'écurie prendrait les devants. Charles partirait trois heures plus tard, au lever de la lune. On enverrait un gamin à sa rencontre, afin de lui montrer le chemin de la ferme et d'ouvrir les clôtures devant lui.

Vers quatre heures du matin, Charles, bien enveloppé dans son manteau, se mit en route pour les Bertaux. Encore endormi par la chaleur du sommeil, il se laissait bercer au trot pacifique de sa bête. Quand elle s'arrêtait d'elle-même devant ces trous entourés d'épines que l'on creuse au bord des sillons, Charles se réveillant en sursaut, se rappelait vite la jambe cassée, et il tâchait de se remettre en mémoire toutes les fractures qu'il savait. La pluie ne tombait plus le jour commençait à venir, et, sur les branches des…

# Madame Bovary

## 2

One night, at about eleven o'clock, they were awoken by the sound of a horse stopping just in front of the door. The maid opened the attic window and conferred for some time with a man who had remained below, in the street. He had come to fetch the doctor; he had a letter. *Nastasie* went down the stairs, shivering, and undid the lock and the bolts one by one. The man left his horse and, following the maid, entered immediately behind her. He drew from inside his gray-tufted wool cap a letter wrapped in a scrap of cloth and presented it delicately to Charles, who leaned his elbow on the pillow to read it. Nastasie, next to the bed, was holding the light. Madame, out of modesty, remained turned toward the space between the bed and the wall, showing her back.

This letter, sealed with a little seal of blue wax, begged Monsieur Bovary to go immediately to the farm called Les Bertaux to set a broken leg. Now, from Tostes to Les Bertaux it is a good six leagues cross-country, going by way of Longueville and Saint-Victor. The night was dark. Madame Bovary the younger was afraid her husband would have an accident. So it was decided that the stableboy would go on ahead. Charles would leave three hours later, when the moon rose. They would send a boy to meet him, to show him the road to the farm and open the gates in front of him.

At about four o'clock in the morning, Charles, well wrapped in his cloak, set off for Les Bertaux. Still drowsy from the warmth of his sleep, he swayed to the peaceful trot of his mare. Whenever she stopped of her own accord in front of one of those holes edged with brambles that farmers dig alongside their furrows, Charles, waking with a start, would quickly recall the broken leg and try to recall what he remembered of all the fractures he knew. The rain was no longer falling; day was beginning to dawn, and on the branches of the leafless apple trees, birds were perched motionless, ruffling their little feathers in the cold morning wind. The flat country spread out as far as the eye could see, and the clumps of trees around the farms formed patches of dark violet at distant intervals on the vast gray surface, which vanished, at the horizon, into the bleak tones of the sky. Charles, from time to time, would open his eyes; then, his mind tiring and sleep returning of itself, he would soon enter a sort of somnolence in which, his recent sensations becoming confused with memories, he would see himself double, at once student and married man, lying in his bed as he had been just now, crossing a surgical ward as in the past. The warm smell of the poultices would mingle in his head with the tart smell of the dew; he would hear the iron rings of the bed curtains running on their rods and his wife sleeping... As he was passing through Vassonville, he saw, by the side of a ditch, a young boy sitting on the grass.

"Are you the doctor?" asked the child.

And at Charles's answer, he took his wooden shoes in his hands and began to run in front of him.

The officer of health, as he went along, learned from what his guide said that Monsieur Rouault must be an extremely well-to-do farmer. He had broken his leg the evening before, as he was returning from *celebrating Twelfth Night* at the home of a neighbor. His wife had been dead for two years. He had only his *young lady* living with him; she helped him run the house.

The ruts became deeper. They were approaching Les Bertaux. The little boy, gliding through a hole in a hedge, disappeared, then reappeared at the far end of a farmyard to open the gate. The horse was slipping on the wet grass; Charles bent low to pass under the branches. The watchdogs in the kennel were barking and pulling on their chains. When he entered Les Bertaux, his horse took fright and shied violently.

It was a prosperous-looking farm. In the stables, one could see, through the open upper halves of the doors, great workhorses feeding tranquilly from new racks.

Along the sides of the buildings extended a large dung heap, steam was rising from it, and, among the hens and turkeys, five or six peacocks were scratching about on top of it, a luxury in a Caux poultry yard. The sheepfold was long, the barn was lofty, with walls as smooth as a hand. In the shed were two large carts and four plows, with their whips, their collars, their full harnesses whose blue wool fleeces were dirtied by the fine dust that fell from the lofts. The yard sloped away upward, planted with symmetrically spaced trees, and the cheerful din of a flock of geese resounded near the pond.

A young woman in a blue merino dress embellished with three flounces came to the door of the house to receive Monsieur Bovary, whom she showed into the kitchen, where a large fire was blazing. The farmhands' breakfast was bubbling all around it, in little pots of unequal sizes. Damp clothes were drying inside the hearth. The fire shovel, the tongs, and the nose of the bellows, all of colossal proportions, shone like polished steel, while along the walls extended an abundant array of kitchen utensils, on which glimmered unevenly the bright flame of the hearth, joined by the first gleams of sunlight coming in through the windowpanes.

Charles went up to the second floor to see the patient. He found him in his bed, sweating under the covers, having hurled his cotton nightcap far away from him. He was a stout little man of fifty, with white skin and blue eyes, bald in front, and wearing earrings. He had by his side, on a chair, a large carafe of eau-de-vie from which he would help himself from time to time to keep up his courage; but as soon as he saw the doctor, his excitement subsided, and instead of swearing as he had been doing for the past twelve hours, he began to groan feebly.

The fracture was simple, without complications of any kind. Charles could not have dared to hope for an easier one. And so, recalling his teachers' manners at the bedsides of the injured, he comforted the patient with all sorts of lively remarks—a surgeon's caresses which are like the oil with which he greases his scalpel. For splints, they went off to fetch, from the cart shed, a bundle of laths. Charles chose one, cut it into pieces, and polished it with a shard of window glass, while the maidservant tore up some sheets to make bandages, and Mademoiselle Emma worked at sewing some pads. She was a long time finding her needle case, and her father grew impatient; she said nothing in response; but, as she sewed, she kept pricking her fingers, which she then raised to her mouth to suck.

Charles was surprised by the whiteness of her fingernails. They were glossy, delicate at the tips, more carefully cleaned than Dieppe ivories, and filed into almond shapes. Yet her hand was not beautiful, not pale enough, perhaps, and a little dry at the phalanges; it was also too long and without soft inflections in its contours. What was beautiful about her was her eyes: although they were brown, they seemed black because of the lashes, and her gaze came to you openly, with a bold candor.

Once the bandaging was done, the doctor was invited by Monsieur Rouault himself to *have a bite* before leaving.

Charles went down into the parlor, on the ground floor. Two places, with silver mugs, were laid there on a little table, at the foot of a large canopied bed hung in calico printed with figures representing Turks. One caught a scent of orrisroot and damp sheets escaping from the tall oak cupboard that faced the window. On the floor, in the corners, stowed upright, were sacks of wheat. This was the overflow from the nearby granary, which one reached by three stone steps. As decoration for the room, there hung from a nail, in the middle of the wall whose green paint was flaking off under the saltpeter, a head of Minerva in black pencil, framed in gilt and bearing on the bottom, written in Gothic letters: "To my dear Papa."

They talked first about the patient, then about the weather they were having, about the severe cold spells, about the wolves that roamed the fields at night. Mademoiselle Rouault did not enjoy herself much at all in the country, especially now that she was almost solely responsible for the care of the farm. Because the room was chilly, she shivered as she ate, revealing her full lips, which she had a habit of biting in her moments of silence.

Her neck rose out of a white, turned-down collar. Her hair, whose two black bands were so smooth they seemed each to be of a single piece, was divided down the middle of her head by a thin part that dipped slightly following the curve of her skull; and just barely revealing the lobes of her ears, it went on to merge in the back in an abundant chignon, with a wavy movement near the temples, which the country doctor noticed for the first time in his life. Her cheeks were pink. She wore, like a man, tucked between two buttons of her bodice, a tortoiseshell lorgnette.

When Charles, after going up to say goodbye to Père Rouault, came back into the parlor before leaving, he found her standing, her forehead against the window, gazing out into the garden, where the beanpoles had been blown down by the wind. She turned around.

"Are you looking for something?" she asked.

"My riding crop, please," he answered.

And he began hunting around on the bed, behind the doors, under the chairs; it had fallen to the floor, between the sacks and the wall. Mademoiselle Emma saw it; she leaned over the sacks of wheat, Charles, gallantly, hurried over, and as he, too, stretched out his arm in the same gesture, he felt his chest brush against the girl's back, stooping beneath him. She straightened up quite red in the face and looked at him over her shoulder, holding out his whip.

Instead of returning to Les Bertaux three days later, as he had promised, he went back the very next day, then twice a week regularly, not counting the unexpected visits he made from time to time, as though by chance.

Everything, moreover, went well; healing progressed according to the book, and when, after forty-six days, Père Rouault was seen trying to walk alone in his poultry yard, people began to consider Monsieur Bovary a man of great ability. Père Rouault said that he would not have been better treated by the foremost doctors of Yvetot or even Rouen.

As for Charles, he did not try to ask himself why he took such pleasure in going to Les Bertaux. Had he thought about it, he would no doubt have attributed his zeal to the gravity of the case, or perhaps to the profit he hoped to make from it. Still, was this why his visits to the farm formed, among all the drab occupations of his life, such a charming exception? On these days he would rise early, set off at a gallop, urge on his animal; then he would dismount to wipe his feet on the grass and put on his black gloves before going in. He liked to find himself arriving at the farmyard, to feel the gate against his shoulder as it turned, and the rooster crowing on the wall, the boys coming to meet him. He liked the barn and the stables; he liked Père Rouault, who would clap him in the palm of the hand, calling him his savior; he liked Mademoiselle Emma's small clogs on the washed flagstones of the kitchen; her raised heels made her a little taller, and when she walked in front of him, the wooden soles, lifting quickly, would clack with a dry sound against the leather of her ankle boots.

She would always see him out as far as the foot of the front steps. When his horse had not yet been brought around, she would stay there. They had said goodbye, they did not go on talking; the fresh air surrounded her, lifting in disarray the stray wisps of hair on the nape of her neck or tossing her apron strings so that they snaked like banners about her hips. Once, during a thaw, the bark of the trees was oozing in the yard, the snow on the tops of the buildings was melting. She was on the doorsill; she went to get her parasol, she opened it. The parasol, of dove-gray iridescent silk, with the sun shining through it, cast moving glimmers of light over the white skin of her face. She was smiling beneath it in the mild warmth; and they could hear the drops of water, one by one, falling on the taut moiré.

During the early days of Charles's visits to Les Bertaux, Madame Bovary the younger never failed to ask after the patient, and she had even, in the double-columned book she kept, chosen for Monsieur Rouault a nice blank page. But when she found out that he had a daughter, she made inquiries; and she learned that Mademoiselle Rouault, raised in a convent, among the Ursulines, had received, as they say, *a fine education*, that she knew, consequently, dancing, geography, drawing, how to do tapestry work and play the piano. That was the limit!

"So," she said to herself, "that's why he has such a smile on his face when he goes to see her, and why he wears his new waistcoat, even though it might get ruined by the rain? Oh, that woman, that woman!..."

And she detested her instinctively. At first she relieved her feelings by making allusions that Charles did not understand; then with the parenthetical remarks that he allowed to pass for fear of a storm; finally with point-blank reproaches that he did not know how to answer.—How was it that he kept going back to Les Bertaux, seeing as Monsieur Rouault was healed and those people hadn't paid yet? Ah! Because there was *a certain person* there, someone who knew how to make small talk, who did embroidery, who had a fine mind. That was what he liked: he wanted young ladies! And she went on:

"Old Rouault's daughter, a young lady! Come now! The grandfather was a shepherd, and they have a cousin who was nearly taken to court for striking a man viciously during a quarrel. She needn't bother to put on such airs, nor show herself at church on Sunday in silk, like a countess. Poor old fellow, anyway—without last year's rapeseed, he'd have had a hard enough time paying his arrears!"

Out of lassitude, Charles stopped going back to Les Bertaux. Héloïse, after much sobbing and many kisses, in a great explosion of love, had made him swear, his hand on his prayer book, that he would not go there anymore. He therefore obeyed; but the boldness of his desire protested against the servility of his behavior, and, with a sort of naïve hypocrisy, he felt that this prohibition against seeing her gave him, in some way, the right to love her. Also, the widow was thin; she had long teeth; in every season she wore a little back shawl whose point hung down between her shoulder blades; her hard body was wrapped in dresses like sheaths that were too short for her and showed her ankles, with the ribbons of her wide shoes crisscrossing over her gray stockings.

Charles's mother would come see them from time to time; but after a few days, it would seem that the daughter-in-law had sharpened her mother-in-law against her own hard edge; and then, like two knives, they would set about scarifying him with their remarks and their observations. He was wrong to eat so much! Why offer a drink to everyone who stopped in? How stubborn not to wear flannel!

It happened that early in the spring, a notary in Ingouville, custodian of the Widow Dubuc's capital, sailed off on a favorable tide, taking away with him all the money in his keeping. Héloïse, it is true, also possessed, besides a share in a ship valued at six thousand francs, her house in the rue Saint-François; and yet, of all that fortune that had been so loudly vaunted, nothing, except a few pieces of furniture and some rags of clothing, had ever appeared in the household. The thing had to be cleared up. The house in Dieppe was found to be riddled with mortgages down to its pilings; what she had placed with the notary, God only knew, and her share in the ship did not amount to more than a thousand ecus. So she had lied, the fine lady! In his anger, the elder Monsieur Bovary, breaking a chair on the flagstones, accused his wife of having brought calamity down upon their son by hitching him to an old nag whose harness wasn't worth her skin. They came to Tostes. They had it out. There were scenes. Héloïse, in tears, throwing herself into her husband's arms, begged him to defend her from his parents. Charles tried to speak up for her. His parents became furious, and they left.

But *the blow had struck home*. A week later, as she was hanging the wash in her yard, she began spitting blood, and the next day, while Charles, his back turned, was at the window closing the curtain, she said: "Oh, my god!," sighed and lost consciousness. She was dead! How astonishing it was!

When everything was over at the cemetery, Charles went back to his house. He found no one downstairs; he went up the second floor, into the bedroom, saw her dress still hanging at the foot of the alcove; then, leaning on the writing desk, he remained there till evening, lost in a sorrowful reverie. She had loved him, after all.

# Two Poems by Xi Chuan

Translated by Lucas Klein from Chinese (China)

Xi Chuan 西川 (the pen-name of Liu Jun 刘军, born in Jiangsu in 1963 but raised in Beijing, where he still lives) is one of contemporary China's most celebrated poets, as well as one of its most hyphenated litterateurs: teacher-essayist-translator-editor-poet. The American writer Eliot Weinberger has described him as a "polymath, equally at home discussing the latest American poetry as Shang Dynasty numismatics."

He is employed at the Central Academy for Fine Arts in Beijing, where he currently teaches pre-modern Chinese literature. Previously, he taught Western literature in Chinese translation, after first being hired as an English-language instructor (he was an English major at Beijing University, and wrote an undergraduate thesis on Ezra Pound's translations from the Chinese). His professional career path follows his poetic development: gaining recognition first as one of the post-Obscure poets in the late '80s, his writing was defined by a condensed lyricism in the Western modernist mode. Today, he writes expansive prose poems that meditate on awkwardness and paradox at the individual and international levels simultaneously. The main shift came in 1989—the year not only of the students' democracy and workers' rights demonstrations, crushed on June 4th in Tiananmen Square, but also of the death of two of Xi Chuan's closest writer-friends Hai Zi 海子 and Luo Yihe 骆一禾 (the former at his own hand)—after which Xi Chuan stopped writing almost completely for three years. When he re-emerged, his form had changed: he was writing a poetry of the anti-lyric, a poetry of contradiction that deconstructed the aestheticism and musicality of his previous self.

The two poems included here represent two distinct points in Xi Chuan's developing style. "Echo" was first written in 1986 and then revised in 1992; its closing line, "turn around, cough up blood, and take up our old trade," could be understood as depicting the decision to start writing again. "Birds" comes from the late '90s and represents Xi Chuan's attempt to find the poetic within the mundane and to describe the poetic in decidedly unpoetic language. His focus on the paradox is one poetic reaction to China's political and economic realities: his writing is at once a reaction to Party phrases such as "People's Democratic Dictatorship" and an affront to the more recent cheapening of cultural knowledge and activity. It is also a particular challenge to translate. Each of his styles, each of his poems, seems to demand a different method, but overall a consistent consideration has motivated my translation: that is, the reader wants to know not only what Xi Chuan says but how he says it, both his images and his style, both his allusions and his elusiveness.

Original text: Xi Chuan, "Hui sheng" from *Xi Chuan de shi*. Beijing: Renmin wenxue chubanshe, 1999; and "Niao" from *Shenqian: Xi Chuan shi wen lu*. Beijing: Zhongguo heping chubanshe, 2006.

# 回声

一个人，犹如一座城市
是一片回声

砖石垒叠而起如层层海浪推远
雾色在清晨和黄昏都很凝重

那些高耸着的钢铁栅栏围护四方
谁曾在其中放牧牛羊？

在木叶相合的地方
男女相遇

在寂寞侵入石头的地方
世界唯回声永存

这蔚蓝色的柱石上

# Echo

a person, like a city,
is the ring of an echo

piled masonry rises like the surge of wave on wave
a monumental fog-color at dawn and at dusk

towering steel railings enclose the perimeter
who has put cattle and sheep to pasture within them?

where leaves meld
man and woman meet

where solitude invades stone
only the echo is eternal

on this sky-blue pillar is woven

一层一层织满铜丝般的藤蔓

在幽暗的房间里
女人采回的果实中有音乐声回旋

我坐在一群老鼠之中
感受到大雪静静地飘落

城上的积雪和高风
把一些人就此埋没——

灵魂化为
子夜峡谷中披衣的守望者

而这里，一片回声
搭起的城市，我们把脚

埋进冰凉的水泥和沙子
转身咳出血痰，重操旧业

storey on storey of lichen like copper wire

inside a dank room
music swirls in the fruit the women have plucked

I sit amidst a herd of mice
and feel the still drift of a snowstorm

the piles of snow and high winds over the city
burying people at this instant—

their spirits change into
cloaked watchmen in the canyon of midnight

but here, a city built by
echoes, we dig our feet

into the ice-cold mud and sand
and turn around, cough up blood, and take up our old trade

# 鸟

鸟是我们凭肉眼所能望见的最高处的生物，有时歌唱，有时诅咒，有时沉默。对于鸟之上的天空，我们一无所知：那里是非理性的王国，巨大无边的虚无；因此鸟是我们理性的边界，是宇宙秩序的支点。据说鸟能望日，至少鹰，作为鸟类之王，能够做到这一点；而假如我们斗胆窥日，一秒钟之后我们便会头晕目眩，六秒钟之后我们便会双目失明。传说宙斯化作一只天鹅与丽达成欢，上帝化作一只鸽子与玛丽亚交配。《诗经》上说："天命玄鸟，降而生商。"尽管有人指出：玄鸟者，鸡巴也，但咱们或可不信。自降为鸟是上帝占有世界的手段，有似人间帝王为微服私访，须扮作他的仆人。因此上帝习惯于屈尊。因此鸟是大地与天空的中介，是横隔在人神之间的桌子，是阶梯，是通道，是半神。鸭嘴兽模仿鸟的外观，蝙蝠模仿鸟的飞翔，而笨重的家禽则堪称"堕落的天使"。我们所歌唱的鸟——它绚丽的羽毛，它轻盈的骨骼——仅仅是鸟的一半。鸟：神秘的生物，形而上的种籽。

# Birds

The bird is the uppermost organism upon which our naked eye can gaze, at times singing, at times cursing, at times silent. As for the sky above the bird, of that we know nothing: it is an irrational kingdom, a vast and boundless void; the bird therefore is the frontier of our rationality, the fulcrum of cosmic order. It has been said that the bird can look directly into the sun, and at least the eagle, king of the avians, can perform this feat; whereas if we peek at the sun for just one second, our heads spin and we see spots, and in six seconds would just go blind. Legend has it that Zeus transformed himself into a swan to ravish Leda, and that God transformed himself into a dove to procreate with Mary. *The Book of Odes* says: "Mandated by Heaven the dark bird / Alighted to bear Shang." While some have pointed out that the aforementioned "dark bird" means *dick,* we don't have to believe this. To descend as a bird is God's method of possessing the world, equivalent to the emperor going incognito to pay visits in the human realm, disguising himself as his own manservant. Ergo, God is accustomed to such condescending. Ergo, the bird is the intermediary between earth and sky, traversing the table between man and spirit, a ladder, a passageway, a demigod. The platypus copies the outward appearance of the bird, the bat copies the bird's flight, and the ungainly poultry may be dubbed some kind of "fallen angel." The bird of our songs—its magnificent plumage, its lissome frame—is but one half of the bird. The bird: mysterious creature, seed of metaphysics.

# Two Poems by Goenawan Mohamad

Translated by Eddin Khoo from Indonesian (Indonesia)

Several poems and essays into the modern Indonesian literary movement, Goenawan Mohamad was hauled into controversy. As a signatory to the Cultural Manifesto of 1963—which opposed the politicization of art and rejected the formal imposition of social realism upon creative endeavour in Indonesia—he encountered his first experience with proscription under the Sukarno regime.

Goenawan Mohamad is renowned as a poet, essayist, and journalist, and remains one of the principal figures in the modern Indonesian literary movement. Among the founders—and long time editor—of the influential news and comment weekly *Tempo* (later forcibly closed by the New Order regime of President Suharto following the events of the Indonesian *Reformasi* movement), he has, with devotion, published on a weekly basis the column *Catatan Pinggir* (Sidelines) which, apart from being greatly influential in his native Indonesia, also blurred the boundaries between poetry, essay, and journalism.

The recipient of several notable awards including, most recently, the Dan David Prize in 2006 for his contributions to journalism, literature, and letters, Goenawan Mohamad straddles Indonesian literature as a figure of paradox—urbane and cosmopolitan in culture and attitude, yet singularly Indonesian, even Javanese in his poetic sensibility. While there has been a steady and consistent evolution in Mohamad's poetry, from early pastoral and landscape renderings to the dense, even apocalyptic vision of his most powerful collection—*Misalkan Kami Di Sarajevo* (As If We Were in Sarajevo)—the sensibility of the witness and "poet as outsider/outcast" has deeply defined his disposition.

"Morning Star" and "At the Flea Market"—both poems from *Misalkan Kami Di Sarajevo*—demonstrate the consummate detail and powers of observation that comprise a Goenawan Mohamad poem. The "poem" as an instrument of eternal questioning and existential contemplation (apparent in both poems) has come to clearly mark the poet's preoccupations. Explorations of religious texts, of commandments, allusions to the tensions which perennially exist between the sacred and the worldly in the poetic interlude have come to dominate his landscape, inspired always by an attitude of moral suspension, cultivated with an astute wielding of (as in Malay) the lack of tense in the Indonesian language and conveyed with the ubiquitous use of the word "perhaps."

In the poetic worldview of Goenawan Mohamad, as he has written himself, "Most important is not the direction, but the courage to discover. Most important is not the conclusion, but the exploration."

Original text: Goenawan Mohamad, from *Misalkan Kita Di Sarajevo*. Jakarta: Kalam, 1998.

# Bintang pagi

Bintang pagi: seperti sebuah sinyal
untuk berhenti. Di udara keras kata-kata berjalan, sejak malam,
dalam tidur: somnambulis pelan, di sayap mega, telanjang,
ke arah tanjung

yang kadang menghilang. Mungkin ada
sebuah prosesi, ke sebuah liang hitam,
di mana hasrat—dan apa saja yang teringat—terhimpun
seperti bangkai burung-burung

di mana tepi mungkin tak ada lagi.
Siapa yang merancangnya, apa yang mengirimnya?
Dari mana? Dari kita? Ada teluk yang tersisih
dan garis lintang yang dihilangkan, barangkali.
Sementara kau dan aku, duduk, bicara,
dalam sal panjang.

# Morning Star

Morning star: like a signal
to stop. In the hard air words venture, through night,
in sleep: somnambulist's pace, on the wings of a cloud, naked,
towards a cape

that sometimes disappears. Perhaps there's
a procession, towards a black hole,
where desire—and all that is remembered—collects
like the carrion of birds

where the precipice may no longer exist.
Who designed it? What delivered it?
From where? From us? There's a cove that's been set apart
and a horizon that's been lost, perhaps.
While you and I sit, speak,
in a broad ward.

Dan aku memintamu: Sebutkan bintang pagi itu,
hentikan kata-kata itu. Beri mereka alamat!

Kau diam. Mungkin ada sejumlah arti yang tak akan hinggap
di perjalanan, atau ada makna, di rimba tuhan,
yang selamanya menunggu tanda hari:
badai, atau gelap, atau—

bukan bintang pagi.

And I ask you: Summon that morning star,
stop that talk. Give it a sign!

You are silent. Perhaps there are meanings that won't be
encountered on this journey, or a purpose, in God's wilderness,
that for eternity, has awaited the break of day;
the storm, the darkness, or—

not the morning star.

# Di pasar loak

Di pasar loak jejak timpa menimpa, menghapus kau dan aku,
mengingat kau mengingat aku.

Pengalaman adalah karpet tua, anakku, pompa-pompa,
gambar buraq, gambar yesus, kamus-kamus, gaun malam dan
hordin panjang, di mana dulu ada sebuah rumah, di mana kita
tak ada, kita tak punya, di mana seekor parkit mungkin
mencoba menyanyi, mencoba menyanyi, dan seseorang tutup
pintu, dengar, papa, aku tak kembali, tak akan kembali

Kenangan adalah seperti manik-manik yang ditawarkan peniup
harmonika itu: butir-butir putih yang teruntai, tak berkait,
sebuah montase, sederet huruf morse, Selamatkan Kami,
Selamatkan Kami, Kami Tenggelam, percintaan yang tak ingin
jadi hantu dalam mimpi malam.

# At the Flea Market

At the flea market footsteps collide, erasing you and I,
remembering you remembering me.

Experience is an old carpet, my child, pumps,
a picture of buraq, picture of Jesus, dictionaries, night gowns and
long drapes, where once there was a house, where we
never were, did not own, where a parakeet perhaps
tried to sing, tried to sing, and someone shut
the door, listen, papa, I won't return, will not return

Memory is like the beads the harmonica player
tenders: strung white grains, unjoined,
a montage, a line of morse code, Save Us,
Save Us, We're Going Down, a love that does not
want to become a ghost in a night dream.

Perpisahan adalah sebuah isyarat kematian, orang tua penjual
kaca itu berkata dan bertanya, siapa kita sebenarnya, mengapa

Parting is a sign of death, the old glass
seller says and asks, who are we really, why

# Two Poems by Oliverio Girondo

Translated by Heather Cleary Wolfgang from Spanish (Argentina)

With his devastating sense of humor, keen eye for detail and sensitivity to the creative potential of language, Oliverio Girondo (1891–1967) helped shape the Latin American avant-garde. Writing prolifically from the 1920s through the mid-1960s, Girondo was at the center of Argentina's cultural life and has been lauded as one of the founding fathers of contemporary Latin American poetry (in the company of Vallejo, Huidobro, Neruda and Paz). Beyond his notorious personal feud with Jorge Luis Borges, Girondo was close with prominent literary figures on both sides of the Atlantic, including Pablo Neruda, Ramón Gómez de la Serna, and Federico García Lorca. So great was the poet's influence that, on the fortieth anniversary of his death, the National Library in Buenos Aires was turned—inside and out—into a monument to his life and work.

Girondo experimented continuously with poetic form, writing both in prose and verse and adopting, in many instances, techniques from the visual arts. In his early work, he plays extensively with the democratization of the poetic form, suggesting that it is not something to be relegated to the ivory tower but rather collected and consumed in the streets. Balancing this idea with his penchant for precise and pointed imagery, he once asserted that a book "should be constructed like a watch and sold like a sausage" (*Notations*, 1926).

"Requiem in Living White," from *Persuasión de los días* (1942), exchanges the playful tone of Girondo's earlier collections for an emotionally bare engagement with the reader that centers on questions of presence, absence, and the process of creative production. The poem is part of a collection that juxtaposes the consumerism and soullessness of the modern city with the immediacy of experience offered by the natural realm. "Tropes," from Girondo's final collection of poems, *En la masmédula* (1956), represents the culmination of the poet's search for the linguistic immediacy of a poetics beyond codified language. By diving headlong into the abstract reaches of neologism and rhythmic experimentation, Girondo creates a work that stretches Spanish to its breaking point, and breathes new life into the modernist tropes of language and the examination of the literary self.

Original text: Oliverio Girondo. "Tropes" from *En la masmédula*. Buenos Aires: Losada, 1953-1956; "Dirge in Living White" from *Persuasión de los días*, Buenos Aires: Losada, 1942.

# Tropos

Toco
toco poros
amarras
calas toco
teclas de nervios
muelles
tejidos que me tocan
cicatrices
cenizas
trópicos vientres toco
solos solos
resacas
estertores
toco y mastoco
y nada

Prefiguras de ausencia
inconsistentes tropos
qué tú
qué qué
qué quenas
qué hondonadas
qué máscaras
qué soledades huecas
qué sí qué no
qué sino que me destempla el toque
qué reflejos
qué fondos
qué materiales brujos
qué llaves
qué ingredientes nocturnos
qué fallebas que no abren
qué nada toco
en todo

# Tropes

I touch
I poke pores
lines
touch tastes
neural lattice
landings
tissues that touch me
scars
ashes
touch tropic paunches
lonely only
excesses
rasps
I palpate and mastócate
and nothing

Harbingers of absence

inconsistent tropes
what you
what what
what whistles
what chasms
what masks
what hollow solitudes
what yes what no
what if not unhinged by a touch
what shadows
what depths
what bewitching elements
what keys
what midnight materials
what cages not unlocked
what naught I touch
in all

# Responso en blanco vivo

Blanca de blanca asfixia
y exangüe blanca vida,
a quien el blanco helado
nevó la blanca mano
de blanca aparecida,
mientras el blanco espanto
blanqueaba su mejilla
de blanca ausencia herida,
al ceñir su blancura
de intacta blanca luna
y blanca despedida.

# Requiem in Living White

White of white suffocation
and bloodless white of life,
covered by the white hand
of white made manifest
snowed down by frozen white,
while all along white terror
was whitening its cheeks
of white and wounded absence,
cinching tight its whiteness
of a chaste white moon
and of white farewell.

# Why You Ought Not to Subscribe to the Newspaper
## *from* Sterility Syndrome

Natalka Sniadanko | Translated by Jennifer Croft from Ukrainian (Ukraine)

Natalka Sniadanko is one of the most vibrant voices in Eastern Europe today. Translated into German, Polish, Russian, and Spanish, Sniadanko is also a translator herself, with such credits as Czesław Miłosz, Günter Grass, and Franz Kafka under her belt. She has received several prestigious residencies and fellowships in both Poland and Germany, and her work is marked by her travels. Ever sharp, ever sensitive, Sniadanko possesses a wit and perspicacity that render each of her sentences sparkling and all of her interests contagious. Her first novel, *Kolekcija prystrastej* (The Passion Collection), funny and touching by turns, tells the story of a young Ukrainian woman falling in love with philology while also experiencing her first crushes and love affairs. Though still under forty, Sniadanko has already published four books in Ukraine since that first, in 2001, and has appeared widely in literary journals and newspapers across Central Europe.

She is a delight for the translator, as much fun to translate as she is to read. Her impeccable style makes it hard to pinpoint any specific difficulty in the translation process. Certain cultural matters, things that are easily recognizable to the Ukrainian reader but totally incomprehensible to the English-speaker, have been briefly explained or, in rare cases, replaced with American cultural approximations. An example is the comparison, early on in this excerpt, of the mail carrier's attitude to that of a police officer who has not received a bribe. Although bribes are still a common enough part of everyday life in some parts of Eastern Europe, I felt that I needed to be a bit more explicit for an American reader, stating the word where it was not mentioned in the original.

Original text: Natalka Sniadanko, *Syndrom Steryl'nosti.* Kharkiv: Folio, 2006.

# Чому не варто передплачувати щоденних газет

Пані Міля, наша поштарка, не любить свою роботу. Не тоді, коли розповідає моїй сусідці пані Оксані, як чоловік Олі з другого поверху, Петро, побив дружину. І "то не в день зарплати, як завжди", а тому, що "застукав їх на гарячому (ви ж знаєте, Оля з Миколою із сусіднього під'їзду тойвово, і вже навіть один раз це саме, ну, ви розумієте, більше трьох тижнів, але нічого, випила "Постінор", і помогло)". Про стосунки Олі й Петра пані Міля знає все, принаймні все, що може знати про такі речі небезпосередній очевидець. І все це вона знає з абсолютно достовірного джерела. Від акушерки Ліди з третього поверху. А звідки знає про це акушерка, пані Міля тактовно замовчує.

Крім того, поштарка завжди в курсі, хто в будинку планує переїжджати і куди саме, які квартири продаються, скільки коштують, коли там востаннє зроблено ремонт. Критичні характеристики усіх маклерів, які працюють із нерухомістю нашого району, також можна почерпнути у нашої поштарки. І якщо їх таки почерпнути, то ви неминуче прийдете до висновку, що у справах нерухомості найкраще звертатися до самої пані Мілі. За її допомогою кільком нашим сусідам уже вдалося вигідно продати і розміняти квартири. Пані Міля розповідає про це з гордістю, не забуваючи щоразу скрушно позітхати, що працювала б вона маклером, то не животіла б на злиденні поштарські копійки. Але не намагайтеся запитати пані Мілю, чому вона не йде працювати маклером, бо вам доведеться вислухати довгу і обурену тираду про те, що вона не з тих, які наживаються чужим коштом, вона звикла чесно заробляти собі на хліб, уся ця купівля-продажа …

# Why You Ought Not to Subscribe to the Newspaper

Milia, our mail carrier, does not enjoy her job. Less so when she's telling my neighbor, Oksana, about how Olia from the second floor's husband, Petro, has just beaten his beloved bride. And "not how he always does, on payday," but because he "caught them in the act (you know, Olia and Mykola from the building next door, you know, she even—once—that was around three weeks ago, but that's done with now, she took something that worked)." Regarding the relationship between Olia and Petro, Milia knows everything, or at least everything anyone can know of such things, being an indirect witness. And everything she knows, she knows from an absolutely secure source. From Lida the midwife, that lives on the third floor. Where the midwife gets her information, Milia tactfully does not divulge.

The mail carrier is also always in the know about who is planning on moving and where they're going, what apartments are up for sale, how much they cost, and when they were last renovated. Critical commentaries on every real estate agent in the region can also be obtained from the mail carrier. These having been obtained, one inevitably comes to the conclusion that in matters of real estate it would be best to skip the agencies and turn directly to Milia herself. It is thanks to her interventions that multiple neighbors have been able to dispense with and acquire apartments so swiftly. Milia talks about this with pride, never neglecting to sigh and say that if she actually worked as an agent she would not be making the pittance she gets from the post office. It is inadvisable, however, to ask Milia why she did not go into real estate: those who do are subjected to a long and indignant tirade on the subject of how Milia does not belong to the brand of people that get rich off other people, of how Milia earns her daily bread honestly, how all that buying, selling, that's not for Milia. Besides, agents live off commissions, and you can never count on that, because what happens if you suddenly can't sell anything, what would you feed the kids with then? At least this way she has a steady, if insignificant, income.

Though she does not enjoy delivering the mail.

Every morning, somewhere between six and six-thirty, I have occasion to see with my own two eyes the aversion Milia has to her profession. For she considers it necessary to actually place in my hands the newspaper—*COLT II*—to which I subscribe.

"Your paper," she proclaims every time, like a police officer giving a driver's license back to someone he's pulled over for a routine check only to find nothing wrong. Now the policeman is forced to let the driver go without a ticket. If such circumstances might be considered at all representative. Perhaps a more realistic version would be that something has in fact been found, but that the driver declines to "just deal with it then and there," to pay a bribe, requesting instead an official ticket. The officer fills out the necessary forms, gazing wistfully at all the cars speeding by that he didn't stop instead, his wrong choice cutting into the family budget.

And to the driver he stops next, he will say, "License and registration please," with the same righteous indignation as Milia bringing me my paper at six in the morning.

To a certain extent I can understand. After all, no one else in the whole building takes the paper. Subscriptions to newspapers went out of fashion ages ago, not only for reasons of thrift, but also due to such phenomena as picking one up at the kiosk on the way or reading it online at the office. This has brought about a significant improvement in the lifestyle of the mail carrier, which is exactly why individual representatives of the post office still required to render an otherwise obsolete service might be forgiven for being a bit indignant. I wouldn't subscribe to anything myself if it weren't for the fact that I really have to read the paper of which I am an editor in the mornings before I go to work so that I'm ready for the morning meeting. Although I haven't explained all of that to Milia. I considered it sufficient to subscribe to the paper at the post office.

"Your paper," grunted the mail carrier today, per tradition, as soon as I opened the door. After the frenzied festivities of the night before, it had been even harder than usual for me to get up. On Milia's face, instead of the impatience I expected, was an almost friendly smile.

"Sign here," said Milia. And instead of the paper, she handed me a police summons.

Milia's dissatisfaction on account of my subscription had taken a passive form only briefly. At first she would toss *COLT II* into my mailbox every day, although she hardly ever managed to do so in the morning. Mostly I would find the paper in my mailbox on my return from work; sometimes I would even catch Milia in the performance of her postal duties. She was unfazed by my timorous entreaty that the paper be delivered in the mornings. In fact, she even suggested that it might be better if she just brought the whole week's worth of papers every Friday, or if she didn't get a chance to some Friday, she would just bring them the next Monday. She also offered to just leave the papers at the post office so that I could, for a modest fee, pick them up myself. "Or," counseled the mail carrier, "why don't you subscribe to some normal thing, with pictures, recipes, things like that. Something that would come once a month. What do you want all that waste paper for?"

I refused. Milia then began to come whenever was convenient for her. Meaning once a week or once every two weeks. I called the head of the postal service. After her boss demanded that she comply with my "whims"—of course a woman with three children, five sectors to work, and a drunk husband *would* see it that way—Milia began waking me up at six o'clock every morning. Meanwhile, I have no right to complain: I'm receiving an additional service, that of having the paper brought up to my apartment and delivered to me in person, at no extra charge.

It's been like that for several months now, and in that time something like mutual understanding has developed between us: she feels a certain satisfaction at the sight of my sleepy face—I never got up that early before—and I get my paper and two extra hours of free time before I start my day. All things considered it's a pretty good arrangement, although not particularly helpful to my perception of the world. It turns out my organism simply cannot get used to getting up so early, which means that I frequently react with severe irritation to things that merit no irritation whatsoever. Between six and seven I am capable of hating the refrigerator for being too loud and, even more so, for not having enough stuff in it. Over the course of the day my irritation undergoes a series of slight modifications, diminishing a little right after a high-calorie lunch or intensifying as a result of not having had lunch. My destructive thoughts about the world often persist clear into evening, and not long ago I realized—much to my horror—that I secretly hated Milia, that I had actually been fantasizing about her being fired or getting sick and going on sick leave, just so long as she ended up not working for the post office anymore. Even if she were to be hit by a car I would not necessarily be that sad about it. One thing was clear: I had to do something immediately.

At the very beginning of the whole thing we tried out being friendly. Milia told me how hard it was to leave the house at five o'clock in the morning when you have three kids. How at the end of your shift your arms and legs hurt, how the postmaster always put you in a bad mood, how hard it was to find a job these days, how often they let mail carriers go. I felt sorry for the poor woman, and I gave her my phone number and told her to call if her kids were sick, and then I would go ahead and go pick up the paper myself. She called the next day. She also called the following day and, in the end, she wound up calling every single day, so that for a month I would go running to the post office to get the newspaper, so as not to let Milia down, although there are kiosks a lot closer to my place. After that she asked me if I could deliver the mail to the neighbors' apartments, then if I could to the people in the neighboring buildings, until finally I figured out that I was going to have to quit my own job soon. Spring was coming, I was going to have to dig up the kitchen garden, pull up the weeds, reap the fruits...

And besides, I didn't have time to read the paper in

the morning any more—I was forced to put it off until evening. As a result the same article was once published two times in a row, and I was severely reprimanded by our editor-in-chief. I then ceased to collect my newspapers from the post office and began to buy them at the kiosk, which infuriated Milia, as my week's worth heap of newspapers had caught the eye of the head of her section who scolded her for it accordingly.

Her triumphant smile today was most likely due to the fact that it was now two-to-one in her favor because, after all, if they locked me up she wouldn't have to deliver the papers anymore.

The water pressure is at its highest in the morning, and it seems like when you turn on the faucet, all the kitchen cabinets are going to come off their hooks. Which is why, when a formidable brownish cascade knocks the little boiling pot out of my hand, scattering coffee grounds on my hands, face, hair, and recently washed walls, it doesn't make much of an impression on me. *Things could be much worse.*

A friend of mine had written that same phrase on the door of his apartment and still maintains that it has helped him through a lot of difficult situations. The events of this morning would no doubt fall into this category: when some monumental pressure forces a brownish liquid out of the faucet at the cost of 1.57 hryvnas per cubic meter, and there's no coffee left.

The ability to not lose hope rarely accompanies me in the morning, before I've drunk my first cup of coffee. But I had a difficult day ahead of me. I could not let myself get upset over trivial things. I had to save my strength.

I dragged myself into the bathroom to wash the coffee off. The water in the shower, equally potent and of a similar color, gradually lost its murkiness until finally I was able to clamber in without being scared. My morning fit of hypochondria was washed away, along with the coffee and fatigue and the usual dirt. Although whether or not the dirt was removed or not I can't say, for even in spite of a real reduction in its initial rusty shade, the water in the shower is never crystal clear. At least not in my town. Water of such a color often has unexpected effects upon hygiene; some people don't bathe for weeks on end, to say nothing of allergies. But things could be much worse.

For example, if you were being called in to the police station. I got out of the shower and read the summons one more time: I was supposed to go in for questioning at noon that day. My weary imagination immediately worked up an explanation in the form of cheap thrillers. Titles like *The Shark and the Throat-Slitters* or *Pissing in Death's Embrace,* or else a postmodernist one like *The Little Princess Kills Bluebeard and Then the Three Little Pigs.* Simple plot: four or five dead bodies, two graphic instances of rape, a case of incest that almost happens but doesn't, a father—the head of the family—who conceals his homosexual attraction to his own son, Siamese twins who turn out to be lesbians at the very end, and a very pregnant killer who uses kung-fu to finish off a local mafia boss just two hours before giving birth to triplets under the wheels of a brand-new Jeep. The umbilical cords are cut by the policeman who arrives on the scene late, as always. And to top it all off, the unavoidable happy ending, enjoyed by everyone who hasn't been murdered.

The shrill sound of the telephone interrupted this morning influx of creativity.

"Just imagine, they think he's been *murdered,*" declared an anxious Snizhana Terpuzhko on the other end of the phone as I tried to adjust to the rapid pace of her speech, so far removed from my own morning mood. Snizhana, the person at our paper in charge of the crime section, continued: "They think he was killed yesterday while we were all still partying. They didn't find the body, but they did find his wallet, along with all his money, his ID, his socks, his suspenders, and his shirt. Of course if you ask me that doesn't really mean anything."

Snizhana fell silent, and more than anything else I was struck by how pleasant that silence was after her uninterrupted monologue. It was only after a minute or so that I began to understand what was going on. "He" was obviously the marketing consultant, Arnold Homosapiens, who had come from Holland at the expense of some foundation and spent two weeks working out a strategy to save our paper from its financial woes. Yesterday Mr. Homosapiens had taken part, along with everyone else, in some binge drinking, and then he must have been abducted, perhaps even killed, because he had disappeared suddenly. Or maybe he had just run away somewhere, leaving behind socks, suspenders, a shirt, an ID, and a wallet with money in it.

The only thing that really stuck out in my mind of all the information contained in that tirade was the suspenders. Why suspenders? The thriller-writer would obviously use that fact, and in the fifth or the tenth chapter would have one of the supporting characters commit suicide with them, said character thereby confessing to having taken part in the kidnapping, perhaps even the killing. Let us suppose that it's one of the two lesbian Siamese twins. One of them, let's just say for now, does the abducting, and the other one doesn't say anything. That unprecedented synchronization serves as the basis for the stress disorder from which they both subsequently suffer. Although that doesn't even answer all the questions. "The Dutch consultant of whom only the suspenders remained" actually sounds genuinely suspicious. Or to be more precise, not suspicious so much as mysterious, or to be more precise still, absurd—like cheese of which only the holes remain. And suspenders do make it sound like foul play. He might have simply forgotten all the other objects: shirt, ID, wallet. Even his socks. He could have just changed his socks and disappeared. But those suspenders, that was just too much.

# Dhaulagiri

Vinod Kumar Shukla | Translated by Arvind Krishna Mehrotra from Hindi (India)

Vinod Kumar Shukla was born in Rajnandgaon, a small town in central India, in 1937. He attended local schools and went to university in Jabalpur, where he studied agricultural science. For most of his working life he taught at Indira Gandhi Agricultural University, Raipur, until he retired as associate professor in 1996. His subject was agricultural extension, which meant traveling to the surrounding villages and acquainting farmers with new agricultural techniques.

His first collection of poems was a 20-page chapbook, *Lagbhag Jaihind* (Hail India, Almost), published in 1971; the ironic title marking him as a new voice in Hindi poetry. These poems were later incorporated into his first full-length book in 1981, mysteriously titled *Voh aadami chala gaya naya naya garam coat pahankar vichar ki tarah* (That Man Put On a New Woolen Coat and Went Away like a Thought).

In "Dhaulagiri," as often in a Shukla poem, the most ordinary things appear other than what they are, making for the constant surprise of his lines. And yet, when it happens, the turn sounds perfectly natural. This surprise that is not a surprise is true particularly of his conclusions, toward which the poem had stealthily been moving all along. "But of course," we catch ourselves saying at the end of "Dhaulagiri," when the sight of the mountain leads to its picture that leads to our ancestors seen in the flesh. In consonance with the ordinariness of the things he writes about, Shukla keeps his language simple. Any difficulties in translating him arise from the unusual ways in which he combines simple words.

Shukla has published two other collections and is working on a novel, his fourth. An English translation of his first novel, *Naukar ki kameez* (*The Servant's Shirt*), was published by Penguin India in 1971, and also made into a film by Mani Kaul.

Original text: Vinod Kumar Shukla, *Sab kuch hona bacha rahega*.
New Delhi: Rajkamal Prakashan, 1992.

# धौलागिरि को देखकर

धौलागिरि को देखकर
मुझे याद आई
धौलागिरि की तस्वीर
क्योंकि तस्वीर पहले देखी गई थी ।

पितामह पूर्वजों के भी चित्र हैं घर में
पूर्वजों को मैंने कभी नहीं देखा
मैं पूर्वजों को नहीं पूर्वजों के चित्र याद करता हूँ ।

लेकिन धौलागिरि को देखने के बाद
मैं अपने पूर्वजों के चित्र नहीं
पूर्वजों को याद करता हूँ ।

# Dhaulagiri

Seeing Mount Dhaulagiri,
I was reminded of its picture,
As I'd seen the picture first.

Among the pictures in my house
Are portraits of my ancestors.
I haven't seen my ancestors,
So whenever I think of them
It's their portraits I think of.

But not after seeing Dhaulagiri.
Now it's the ancestors who come to mind
And not their likenesses.

# Birds in the Mouth

Samanta Schweblin | Translated by Joel Streicker from Spanish (Argentina)

Samanta Schweblin published the acclaimed collection of short stories, *El núcleo del disturbio,* in 2001, at the age of twenty-two. Her eagerly awaited second collection, *Pájaros en la boca*, the title story of which is presented here, was published in 2008 and won the prestigious Casa de las Américas Prize.

Schweblin's stories reside on the ambiguous frontier between realism and the fantastic. The precision of the prose and the straightforward thrust of the plots create a realistic world in which the oddest events nonetheless seem utterly natural. At the same time, her stories call into question the taken-for-granted character of our everyday experience. Schweblin's work is also often marked by characters who seem destined to expend tremendous effort to exert control over their worlds, with the most surprising of results.

Perhaps Schweblin's preoccupation with the thin line separating reality and fantasy, and with control, is the product of a society coming to grips with the legacy of a dictatorship that tried brutally to bend society to its particular version of reality. The torture and disappearances—the abuses widely known in their time yet officially unacknowledged until the fall of the dictatorship—also shape a sensibility in which the ordinary rules of life are held in suspense, in which the mundane cedes to the strange, the horrible, and the obscene. While other young Argentine writers, such as Félix Bruzzone, approach this sensibility in their work, Schweblin wholeheartedly, and inimitably, embraces it.

The challenge in translating this story lies in capturing the deceptively clear rhythm that lulls the reader into accepting the plausibility of the implausible, the naturalness of the unnatural. As with all of Schweblin's work, the story threatens to betray the strange conceit on which it is built, yet never quite does. It is like an enormous drop of water on the verge of bursting and dissolving into many small drops, yet somehow remaining intact, its tensile strength stretched almost to the breaking point.

Original text: Samanta Schweblin, *Pájaros en la boca*. Buenos Aires: Planeta-Emecé, 2009.

# Pájaros en la boca

Apagué el televisor y miré por la ventana. El auto de Silvia estaba estacionado frente a la casa, con las balizas puestas. Pensé si había alguna posibilidad real de no atender, pero el timbre volvió a sonar: ella sabía que yo estaba en casa. Fui hasta la puerta y abrí.

–Silvia –dije.

–Hola –dijo ella, y entró sin que yo alcanzara a decir nada–. Tenemos que hablar.

Señaló el sillón y yo obedecí, porque a veces, cuando el pasado toca a la puerta y me trata como hace cuatro años atrás, sigo siendo un imbécil.

–No va a gustarte. Es... Es fuerte –miró su reloj–. Es sobre Sara.

–Siempre es sobre Sara –dije.

–Vas a decir que exagero, que soy una loca, todo ese asunto. Pero hoy no hay tiempo. Te venís a casa ahora mismo, esto tenés que verlo con tus propios ojos.

–¿Qué pasa?

–Además le dije a Sara que ibas a ir, así que te espera.

Nos quedamos en silencio un momento. Pensé en cuál sería el próximo paso, hasta que ella frunció el seño, se levantó y fue hasta la puerta. Tomé mi abrigo y salí tras ella.

Por fuera la casa se veía como siempre, con el césped recién cortado y las azaleas de Silvia colgando de los balcones del primer piso. Cada uno bajó de su auto y entramos sin hablar. Sara estaba en el sillón. Aunque ya había terminado las clases por ese año, llevaba puesto el jumper de la secundaria, que le quedaba como a esas colegialas porno de las revistas. Estaba sentada con la espalda recta, las rodillas juntas y las manos sobre las rodillas ...

# Birds in the Mouth

I turned off the TV and looked out the window. Silvia's car was parked in front of the house with the emergency lights on. I wondered if there was a real possibility of not answering the door, but the bell rang again; she knew I was home. I went to the door and opened it.

"Silvia," I said.

"Hi," she said, and entered without my managing to say anything. "We have to talk."

She pointed to the sofa and I obeyed because, sometimes, when the past knocks on the door and treats me like it did four years before, I continue to be an idiot.

"You're not going to like it. It's…it's hard," she looked at her watch. "It's about Sara."

"It's always about Sara," I said.

"You're going to say I'm exaggerating, that I'm nuts, all that kind of stuff. But there's no time today. You're coming home right now, this you have to see with your own eyes."

"What's going on?"

"Besides, I told Sara that you were going to come, so she's waiting for you."

We remained silent for a moment. I thought about what the next step would be, until she frowned, got up and went to the door. I grabbed my coat and went out after her.

Outside the house looked as it always did, with the lawn recently cut and Silvia's azaleas hanging from the balconies on the second floor. We each got out of our cars and went in without speaking. Sara was on the sofa. Although classes were out for the year, she was wearing her middle school uniform, which fit her like the ones on schoolgirls in porn magazines. She was sitting with her back straight, her knees together and her hands on them, concentrating on some point on the window or in the garden, as if she were doing one of those yoga exercises of her mother's. I realized that, although she had always been rather pale and skinny, she looked brimming with health. Her legs and arms seemed stronger, as if she had been exercising for a few months. Her hair shone and her cheeks were slightly pink, as if they were painted, only this was real. When she saw me enter she smiled and said:

"Hi, Daddy."

My girl was a real sweetheart, but those two words were enough for me to understand that something was wrong with that kid, something surely related to her mother. Sometimes I think that maybe I should have taken her with me, but almost always I think not. A few yards from the TV, next to the window, there was a cage. It was a birdcage—some two, two and a half feet tall—hanging from the ceiling, empty.

"What's that?"

"A cage," said Sara, and smiled.

Silvia gestured to me to follow her to the kitchen. We went to the picture window and she turned around to make sure that Sara was not listening to us. She remained sitting up straight on the sofa, looking toward the street, as if we had never arrived. Silvia spoke to me in a low voice.

"Look, you're going to have to take this calmly."

"Quit jerking me around. What's going on?"

"I haven't given her any food since yesterday."

"Are you kidding?"

"So you can see it with your own eyes."

"Uh-huh... Are you nuts?"

She said that we should return to the living room and she pointed to a chair. I sat in front of Sara. Silvia left the house and I saw her cross in front of the picture window and enter the garage.

"What's up with your mother?"

Sara shrugged her shoulders, leading me to understand that she didn't know. Her black, straight hair was tied in a ponytail, with bangs that fell almost to her eyes. Silvia returned with a shoebox. She held it straight, with both hands, as if it were something delicate. She went to the cage, opened it, took from the box a very small sparrow, the size of a golf ball, stuck it in the cage and closed it. She threw the box on the floor and kicked it aside, together with nine or ten similar boxes that were piled up under the desk. Then Sara got up, her pony tail shining on one side and then the other of the back of her neck, and she went to the cage, skipping, like little girls five years younger than her do. Her back to us, rising up on tiptoes, she opened the cage and took out the bird. I couldn't see what she did. The bird screeched and she struggled a moment, perhaps because the bird tried to escape. Silvia covered her mouth with her hand. When Sara turned toward us the bird was no longer there. Her mouth, nose, chin, and both hands were stained with blood. She smiled, ashamed, her giant mouth arched and opened, and her red teeth forced me to jump up. I ran to the bathroom, locked myself in and vomited in the toilet. I thought that Silvia would follow me and start in with the blaming and the ordering around from the other side of the door, but she didn't. I washed my mouth and face, and I stood listening in front of the mirror. They were taking something heavy down from the floor above. They opened and closed the front door a few times. Sara asked if she could take a photo from the mantelpiece with her. When Silvia answered that she could her voice was already far away. I opened the door trying not to make noise, and I looked out into the hall. The main door was wide open and Silvia was loading the cage in the back seat of my car. I took a few steps, with the intention of leaving the house while yelling a few choice words at her, but Sara left the kitchen and went toward the street and I stopped cold so that she would not see me. They hugged. Silvia kissed her and put her in the passenger seat. I waited until she returned and closed the door.

"What the fuck…?"

"You take her," she went to the desk and began to crush and fold the empty boxes.

"My God, Silvia, your daughter eats birds!"

"I can't take any more."

"She eats birds! Is she out of her mind? What the fuck does she do with the bones?"

Silvia looked at me, disconcerted.

"I suppose she swallows them, too. I don't know if birds…" she said and stood there looking at me.

"I can't take her with me."

"If she stays here I'll kill myself. I'll kill myself and first I'll kill her."

"She eats birds!"

Silvia went to the bathroom and locked herself in. I looked outside, through the picture window. Sara waved to me happily from the car. I tried to calm myself. I thought about things that would help me take a few clumsy steps toward the door, praying that in that time I would manage to turn back into a normal human being, a tidy and organized guy capable of standing for ten minutes in front of the canned goods shelves at the supermarket, corroborating that the beans he's taking are the proper ones. I thought about things like if we know that some people eat people then eating live birds isn't so bad. Also, from a health perspective it's better than drugs, and from a social perspective it's easier to hide than a pregnancy at age thirteen. But I think that even the car doorhandle kept repeating *she eats birds, she eats birds, she eats birds,* and so on.

I took Sara home. She didn't say anything on the way and when we arrived she took her things out by herself. Her cage, her suitcase—which they had put in the trunk—and four shoeboxes like the one that Silvia had brought from the garage. I wasn't able to help her with anything. I opened the door and waited there for her to go and come with everything. When we went in, I indicated that she could use the upstairs room. After she settled in, I made her come down and sit in front of me, at the dining room table. I prepared two cups of coffee but Sara moved her cup aside and said that she didn't drink infusions.

"You eat birds, Sara," I said.

"Yes, Daddy."

She bit her lips, ashamed, and said:

"You, too."

"You eat *live* birds, Sara."

"Yes, Daddy."

I remembered Sara at age five, sitting at the table across from us, her head no higher than her plate, fanatically devouring a squash, and I thought that, somehow, we would have to solve the problem. But when the Sara I had in front of me smiled again, I asked myself what it would feel like to swallow something warm and moving, to have something full of feathers and feet in your mouth, and I covered up my own mouth with my hand, like Silvia did, and I left her alone before the two untouched cups of coffee.

Three days went by. Sara was in the living room almost all the time, sitting up straight on the sofa with her knees together and her hands on them. I went out early to work and I spent hours searching the Internet for infinite combinations of the words "bird," "raw," "cure," "adoption," knowing that she kept sitting there, looking out toward the garden for hours. When I would enter the house, around seven o'clock, and see her just as I had imagined her the whole day, the hair would stand up on the back of my neck and I had an urge to rush out and leave her locked inside, hermetically sealed, like those insects one hunts as a kid and keeps in glass jars until the air gives out. Could I do it? When I was a kid I saw a bearded woman at the circus who put mice in her mouth. She held them there a while, with the tail moving between her closed lips, while she walked before the audience smiling and rolling her eyes back in her head, as if it gave her great pleasure. Now, I thought about that woman almost every night, tossing in my bed without being able to sleep, considering the possibility of putting Sara in a mental hospital. Maybe I could visit her once or twice a week. Silvia and I could take turns. I thought of those cases in which doctors suggest isolating the patient, distancing him from the family for a few months. Perhaps it was a good option for everyone, but I wasn't sure that Sara could survive a place like that. Or maybe she could. In any case, her mother wouldn't permit it. Or maybe she would. I couldn't decide.

On the fourth day Silvia came to see us. She brought five shoeboxes, which she left beside the front door, just inside. Neither of us said anything about it. She asked about Sara and I pointed to the upstairs room. When she came down, I offered her a cup of coffee. We drank in the living room, in silence. She was pale and her hands trembled so much that they made the china rattle each time she set the cup on the saucer. Each knew what the other was thinking. I could say "this is your fault, this is what you accomplished," and she could say something absurd like "this is what happens because you never paid attention to her." But the truth is that we were already very tired.

"I'll take care of this," said Silvia before leaving, pointing to the shoeboxes. I didn't say anything, but I was profoundly grateful.

In the supermarket people loaded their carts with cereal, candy, vegetables, meat, and dairy products. I limited myself to my canned goods and I waited in line in silence. I went two or three times a week. Sometimes, even though I didn't need to buy anything, I would stop by before going home. I would take a cart and walk down the aisles thinking about what I might be forgetting. At night we would watch TV together. Sara, erect, sitting on her corner of the sofa, me on the other end, spying on her every once in a while to see if she was following the program or if she had her eyes fixed on the garden again. I prepared food for the two of us and carried it to the living room on two trays. I would leave Sara's in front of her, and there it stayed. She would wait until I began to eat and then she would say:

"Excuse me, Daddy."

She would get up, go to her room and delicately close her door. The first time I lowered the volume on the TV and waited in silence. A sharp, short screech was heard. A few second later the faucets and the water running. Sometimes she would come down a few minutes later, perfectly combed and peaceful. Sometimes she would take a shower and come down already in her pajamas.

Sara didn't want to go outside. Studying her behavior I thought that perhaps she suffered from the beginnings of agoraphobia. Sometimes I would take a chair into the garden and try to convince her to go out a while. But it was useless. She retained, nevertheless, a skin radiant with energy and every day she looked more beautiful, as if she spent the day exercising in the sun. Every so often, going about my business, I would find a feather. On the floor next to the dining room door, behind the coffee can, among the silverware, still damp in the bathroom sink. I would pick them up, careful so that she wouldn't see me doing it, and throw them in the toilet. Sometimes I would stand there watching how they went down with the water. Sometimes the toilet would fill up again, the water would settle, like a mirror again, and I would still be there watching, thinking about whether it would be necessary to go back to the supermarket, about whether filling the carts with so much junk was really justified, thinking about Sara, about what it was that was in the garden.

One afternoon Silvia called to let me know that she was in bed with a ferocious flu. She said that she couldn't visit us. She asked me if I could manage without her and then I understood that *not being able to visit us* meant *that she couldn't bring more boxes*. I asked her if she had a fever, if she was eating well, if she had seen a doctor, and when I had her sufficiently occupied with these answers I said that I had to hang up and I hung up. The phone rang again, but I didn't answer it. We watched TV. When I brought my food Sara didn't get up to go to her room. She looked at the garden until I was done eating, and only then did she return to the program that we were watching.

The next day, before returning home, I passed by the supermarket. I put a few things in my cart, the same as always. I walked down the aisles as if I were making a reconnaissance of the supermarket for the first time. I stopped in the pet section, where there was food for dogs, cats, rabbits, birds and fish. I picked up a few packages of food to see what they were. I read what ingredients they were made of, the calories they supplied and the amounts that were recommended for each breed, weight and age. Afterwards I went to the gardening section, where there were only plants with or without flowers, flower pots and dirt, so I returned again to the pet section and I stood there thinking what I was going to do later. People filled their carts and dodged around me. A sale on dairy products for Mother's Day was announced on the loudspeakers and then they played a melodious song about a guy who had a lot of women but missed his first love, until I finally pushed my cart and returned to the canned goods section.

That night Sara took a while to fall asleep. My room was below hers, and I heard her through the ceiling walk nervously, lie down, get up again. I asked myself what condition her room must be in; I had not gone up there since she had arrived. Perhaps the place was a real disaster, a corral filled with filth and feathers.

The third night after Silvia's call, before returning home, I stopped to see the cages of birds that were hanging from the awning of a pet shop. None looked like the sparrow that I had seen at Silvia's house. They were colorful, and in general they were a little bigger. I was there for a while, until a salesman came up to ask me if I was interested in a bird. I said no, absolutely not, that I was just looking. He stayed close by, moving boxes, looking down the street, until he understood that I really wasn't going to buy anything, and returned to the counter.

At home, Sara waited on the sofa, sitting up straight in her yoga position. We said hello.

"Hi, Sara."

"Hi, Dad."

She was losing her rosy cheeks and she no longer looked as well as before. I made my dinner, sat on the sofa, and turned on the TV. After a while Sara said:

"Daddy..."

I swallowed what I was chewing and turned the volume down, doubting that she had really spoken to me, but there she was, with her knees together and her hands on them, watching me.

"What?" I said.

"Do you love me?"

I made a gesture with my hand, accompanied by a nod. Everything together meant that, yes, of course I do. She was my daughter, wasn't she? And even then, just in case, thinking in particular of what my ex-wife would have considered "the right thing," I said:

"Yes, sweetie. Of course."

And then Sara smiled, once more, and looked at the garden during the rest of the show.

We slept poorly again, she pacing from one end of the bedroom to the other, me tossing in my bed until I fell asleep. The next morning I called Silvia. It was Saturday, but she didn't answer the phone. I called later, and around noon as well. I left a message, but she didn't answer. Sara spent the whole morning sitting on the sofa, looking at the garden. Her hair was a little messy and she was no longer sitting so straight; she seemed very tired. I asked her if she was doing okay and she said:

"Yes, Dad."

"Why don't you go out to the garden for a little bit?"

"No, Dad."

Thinking about the conversation the night before, it occurred to me that I could ask her if she loved me, but immediately it seemed to me a stupid idea. I called Silvia again. I left another message. In a low voice, taking care so that Sara wouldn't hear me, I said on the machine:

"It's urgent, please."

We waited, each of us sitting on his end of the sofa, with the TV on. A few hours later Sara said:

"Excuse me, Dad."

She shut herself up in her room. I turned off the TV to hear better: Sara didn't make a sound. I decided to call Silvia one more time. But I picked up the phone, listened to the dial tone, and hung up. I took the car to the pet shop, looked for the salesman and told him that I needed a small bird, the smallest he had. The salesman opened a catalogue of photos and said that the prices and food varied from species to species.

"Do you like exotic ones or do you prefer something more domestic?"

I smacked the countertop with the palm of my hand. A few things on top of the counter jumped and the salesman remained silent, looking at me. I pointed to a small, dark bird, which moved nervously from one side of its cage to the other. They charged me one hundred and twenty pesos and gave it to me in a square box made out of green cardboard, with little holes punched around, a free bag of birdseed that I didn't accept, and a flyer from the breeder with a photo of the bird on the front.

When I returned, Sara remained shut in. For the first time since she was at home I went up and entered her room. She was seated on the bed in front of the open window. She looked at me, but neither of us said anything. She looked so pale that she seemed sick. The room was clean and orderly, the door to the bathroom half open. There were some twenty shoeboxes on the desk, but broken down—so that they wouldn't take up so much space—and piled carefully one on top of the other. The cage hung empty near the window. On the little night table, next to the lamp, was the framed picture that she had taken from her mother's house. The bird moved and its feet could be heard against the cardboard, but Sara remained immobile. I left the box on top of the desk and, without saying anything, I left the room and closed the door. Then I realized that I didn't feel well. I leaned against the wall to rest for a moment. I looked at the breeder's flyer, which I still carried in my hand. On the back was information about care of the bird and its procreation cycles. It emphasized the need for the species to be paired during mating periods and the things that could be done to make its years of captivity as pleasant as possible. I listened to a brief screech, and then the faucet of the bathroom sink. When the water began to run I felt a little better and knew that, somehow, I would figure out a way to get down the stairs.

# Two Poems by Latiff Mohidin

Translated by Eddin Khoo from Malay (Malaysia)

Traditional oral poetic forms, including the *pantun* (pantoum) and *mentera* (incantation), were principal influences in the beginnings of modern Malay poetry. Adopted by modern poets as an expression of cultural fidelity, but used to address contemporary social themes, traditional forms defined the patterns, meter, and aesthetics of modern Malay poetry.

Latiff Mohidin, widely acknowledged as being a formative figure in the creation of a new aesthetic in art and poetry in the Malay language, belonged to a generation of poets—rising in the 1970s—who departed from the strict stance of social realism adopted by preceding Malaysian poets. Having obtained a formal education in fine art in Germany, he returned from Europe imbued with the poetics of Rimbaud, Rilke, Baudelaire, and Verlaine, traveled the Southeast Asian region at the height of the Vietnam War, and produced a series of paintings, *Pago-Pago,* and a collection of poems *Sungai Mekong* (Mekong River) that came to serve as hallmarks in the development of abstraction in Malaysian art and introduced a "radical voice" in Malay poetics.

To encapsulate the poetry of Latiff Mohidin simply within the context of "departures" and the "radical" would, however, be disingenuous. Within the nascent Malaysian critical tradition—still largely affected by the attitudes of social realism—the poetry of Latiff Mohidin is principally regarded as belonging to the realms of the esoteric or, in Malay parlance, *kabur* (obscure). Yet, in his spirit, diction, and symbolism, he has served as a confluence between the sensibilities of the "traditional" and the tendencies of the modernist. Rooted in the old Malay spirit of *kembara* (wandering), the poetry of Latiff Mohidin remains expansive in its poetic allusions and diverse in its imagery.

The poems "The Calm Has Brought the Storm" and "Poems of the Deep Night" remain highly representative of the poet's progression in form, style, and poetic concern. Paradox, the sensual, and an almost epigrammatic delivery are recurrent themes in the poet's evolution. In both of these poems—distinct in their themes—concentrated imagery yields to a capaciousness of spirit and poetic possibility. Harnessed by the lack of tenses in the Malay language, the translation naturally bequeaths the poems a sense of the timeless and transcendent.

"A poem," Latiff Mohidin writes, "is not a project, it is not a shirt or a pair of shoes or an advertisement that must be adapted… A poet as an artist does not require a compulsion beyond *the* compulsion: to demonstrate truth, to convey sincerity and honesty, elevate aesthetics into the beauty of the transcendent, to possess imaginative and creative energies in novel situations, to bring purity and harmony, deliver awareness while unaware; most importantly, to remind…"

Original text: Latiff Mohidin, "Poems of the Deep Night" from *Pesisir Waktu*. Kuala Lumpur: Dewan Bahasa dan Pustaka, 1981; and "The Calm Has Brought the Storm" from *Serpihan Dari Pendalaman*. Kuala Lumpur: Private Publication, 1979.

# Sajak-sajak tengah malam

I

malam ini
    bulan
telah membuka
tirai emasnya
    ombak
telah membuka
bibir merahnya
mereka bertemu di sini
di lereng pinggangmu
untuk menyaksikan
    tarian asyikmu
    tarian mautku

II

kau lihat bagaimana
    kusapu alismu
        dengan manisan
kulihat bagaimana
    semut mabuk
        di lengkung alismu
            beriringan

III

dari kerongkongmu
yang sepi
kudengar
serigala meraung

# Poems of the Deep Night

I

this night
the moon
unfurls
its golden curtain
the wave opens
its red lips
they come together here
on the slant of your waist
to witness
your dance of ardour
my dance of death

II

you look at how
i graze your eyebrows
with sweetness
i look at how
the ants intoxicate
at the arc of your eyebrows
in procession

III

from your silent
throat
you hear
the wolves howl

kuda meringkik
singa menderam
— tiada hentinya

dan halkumku
turun naik
semakin keras
menyahut pekikan
kerongkongmu

### IV

pahamu:
          kacip yang
lembut

### V

tujuh lautan
satu gelombag
   di pusar perutmu
   berpusing
denyutan purba
memanggil namaku
   kuturuni bukit
   kutinggalkan padang luas

aku merangkak kembali
ke lubuk kelamu

the horses whine
the lions roar
—incessantly

and my adam's apple
rises and falls
hardens
answers the scream
of your throat

### IV

your thighs:
    soft
scissors

### V

seven seas
a single wave
  on the navel of your belly
  undulating
an ancient pulse
calls my name
  i descend from the hill
  i leave the open field

i crawl back
into the depths of your darkness

# Tenang telah membawa resah

*buat Uda*

tenang telah membawa resah
resah telah membawa
kau ke mari
kau telah memilih
untuk tidak tinggal diam
setiap yang kau pegang
terasa lama
setiap yang kau jauhi
terasa dekat
waktu pintu tertutup
kau ingin keluar
waktu ruang terbuka
kau ingin duduk
kau duduk untuk berdiri
bungkusan yang kau buka
kau ikat kembali
yang kau pinta kau tolak
yang kau jerat kau lepaskan
setelah patuh kau engkar
setelah menang kau mengalah

tenang telah membawa resah
resah telah membawa
kau ke mari
tapi kamarmu bukan di sini
dan kau merantau lagi

# The Calm Has Brought the Storm

*for Uda*

the calm has brought the storm
the storm has brought
you here
you have chosen
to not live still
all that you hold
feels old
all you've forsaken
feels near
when doors are shut
you want to leave
when space is opened
you want to sit
you sit to stand
the parcel you opened
you bind again

all you request you refuse
all you snare you set free
having conformed you renounce
having won you surrender

the calm has brought the storm
the storm has brought
you here
but your room is not here
and you wander once again

# Turn in the River

Andrey Dmitriev | Translated by Henry Whittlesey from Russian (Russia)

What if a young, sick Andrey hid on a ledge over beetling cliffs? His father, the police, the school matrons are looking for him, but he promised the head doctor he'd hide (so his dad won't take him away). Maybe that ledge is even the boy's favorite spot: little Andrey has been released from the stifling claustrophobia of his home in a bleak provincial city; he sits atop a mountain and is free to let his thoughts soar over the river, forest, and countryside beyond. No parents arguing, no classmates to tease him, nothing but peace as *he carefully walks on the waves, listening to the dense sweltering air, peering into the trembling dove-covered mirage hiding the horizon, and asking who knows who: am I going the right way? Is it right that I am going? Am I allowed to go that far alone?*

Or did Andrey become the head doctor at the TB boarding school on the mountain? Well, he probably didn't do that, because Andrey Dmitriev, born in St. Petersburg, raised in Pskov and Moscow, studied cinematography in the capital and has written narratives and scripts ever since. But in this novella, the little boy and head doctor have to negotiate conflicts recurring frequently enough in Dmitriev's work to conclude that the author himself has intimate experience with the fate of such torn protagonists. That is about the best I can give you in the way of biographical information to pique your curiosity. Otherwise, he lives both in Moscow off the main road from Sheremetyevo Airport to the Kremlin and in a village four hours north of the capital.

*Turn in the River* interweaves the aforementioned plot of a boy hiding on a mountain ledge with a born-again Christian (woman) visiting a cathedral next to the school. The critically acclaimed novella is also the second part of a loose diptych with *Voskoboev and Elizaveta* (published by Arch Literary Journal, 2009), with pessimism and urban squalor yielding to optimism and spiritual regeneration. Whereas the earlier protagonists blew themselves up (*Voskoboev and Elizaveta*) or were sent (back) to jail (*Steps* and *Golubev*), here they reject materialism, walk on waves, and implicitly save lives.

Andrey Dmitriev has been conferred the Apollon Grigorev award for his novel *The Road Back,* and *Turn in the River* was shortlisted for the Russian Booker prize. Many novellas and stories have been published in prominent Russian literary journals (*Novyi Mir, Znamya,* etc.) and in florilegia from the publishing house Vagrius. Translated into German, French, Czech and English, he is currently writing his third novel.

Original text: Andrey Dmitriev, *Doroga obratno.* Moscow: Vagrius, 2003.

# Поворот реки

– Смирнов!—тормошит главный врач спящего мальчика.—Смирнов!—шепчет Снетков, боясь разбудить остальных детей.—Одевайся, Смирнов. И не забудь пальто.

Мертвый час. На горе безмолвно, лишь из пищеблока слышен шум воды и гром дюраля... Мальчик покорно идет по двору следом за главным врачом, просыпаясь на ходу и без боязни гадая, ради какой процедуры его подняли: ради такой, когда больно, или для такой, когда всего лишь холодно и щекотно от чужих внимательных прикосновений... С крыльца округлого, приземистого собора, силуэт которого, размноженный на миллионах открыток, уже успел наскучить почтальонам, поднимаются двое чужик: мужчина в серой драповой куртке и женщина в черном плаще.

– Простите, давно здесь заперто?—спрашивает мужина.

– Здесь всегда заперто,—привычно и сухо отвечает Снетков, не останавливаясь.— Обратитесь к сторожу. Видели дом справа от ворот, как вошли? Он должен быть там.

– Может, вы нам откроете?—неуверенно просит женщина.

– Это музей. А мы—интернат. Мы не имеем к этому ни малейшего отношения.—Снетков берет мальчика за руку и, обогнув собор, затем обрубленную колокольню, ведет его не в амбулаторию, а подальше от случайных глаз—в пустой школьный корпус, насквозь пропахший дезинфекцией, печным перегаром и мокрой тряпкой. Закрывшись в учительской и плотно сдвинув на окне лиловые шторы ...

# Turn in the River

"Smirnov!" the head doctor jiggles the sleeping boy. "Smirnov!" whispers Snetkov, afraid of waking the other children. "Get dressed, Smirnov. And don't forget your coat."

Rest hour. It is still on the mountain; all you can hear is the sound of water and the banging of duraluminum from the cafeteria... The boy obediently follows the head doctor through the yard, waking up along the way and bravely guessing what kind of procedure they roused him for: the kind where it hurts, or the one where it's just cold and tickles at a stranger's careful touch... From the veranda of the round stumpy cathedral, whose silhouette has been reproduced on millions of postcards and already bores the mailmen, two strangers ascend: a man in a thick gray wool jacket and a woman in a black raincoat.

"Excuse me, has it been locked up for a long time?" asks the man.

"It's always locked up," Snetkov replies normally and dryly, without stopping. "Talk to the caretaker. Did you see the house to the right of the gate when you came in?.. He should be in there."

"Maybe you could let us in?" requests the woman uncertainly.

"That's a museum. We're a boarding school. We don't have anything to do with that." Snetkov takes the boy by the hand and, after skirting the cathedral, then the lopped off belfry, leads him not to the clinic, but a little farther from stray eyes—into the empty school building, thoroughly permeated by disinfectant, stove fumes and wet rags. After closing the door to the teachers' room and pulling the lilac curtains shut, Snetkov sits opposite the boy at a heavy table covered with a threadbare tablecloth and swamped by colorless notebooks in cellophane wrappers.

"How are you, Smirnov?"

"Okay."

"Did you eat well today?"

The boy is silent.

"Did you at least eat something today?"

"I ate the purée stuff."

"Purée isn't enough." Snetkov shakes his head. "You need to eat everything. How else will you become strong? If you don't eat, you'll stay sick."

"I won't do it any more."

"Won't do what?"

"I won't eat only a little."

"Ugh, I'm not talking about that, Smirnov!" the head doctor cries out, frustrated. "I—I wanted to talk with you… Do you remember, in April, when your father came and took you away?.. He said it sort of looked like your mommy was going to leave you all; but if she saw you in front of her, she would think twice about leaving?.. I'm talking to you—excuse me—like a man to a man… Do you remember?"

"Yes…"

"He checked you out and brought you back a month later—and how were you then? You, Smirnov, were simply emaciated. You slept poorly: screamed… Lost weight… Worst of all, your TB began to stir, your TB, Smirnov! We were barely able to correct it."

"Did she leave?"

"Did I say she left?!" said Snetkov frustrated. "No, nothing of the sort! I just wanted to tell you: your father has come again, wants to take you away again. But you, Smirnov, don't need their arguments now. You don't need anxiety and adversity at all."

"Is he here?"

"He will be shortly. With the police, if he isn't lying… If they can't find you on their own, I won't tell them anything… What do you think, Smirnov?"

The boy is silent.

"Don't cry; that's the main thing. I understand it all perfectly: you probably miss your father. And your mother."

"Yes."

"But of course!" Snetkov sighs and moans sadly. "It's

just simply impossible for you to go with them. You'll return like a rag again—and what will you have us do with you then?... Let them make up on their own somehow and bring you presents. And in one little year I'll release you forever. What is one little year! One little year is a trifle, you won't even notice it... Won't notice it, Smirnov?"

"Won't notice it..."

"That's right... Tell me honestly," Snetkov winks clumsily, "do you have a secret little spot on our territory or somewhere close to our territory?.. I know, after all, that each of you has his own little hiding place for games."

The boy looks away.

"Could you, Smirnov, while everyone is sleeping, hide so no one would know where you are or be able to find you, so not even I would know, so I won't have to lie to them? And when it's okay to come out, I'll call for you loudly. Or I'll tell Vinogradov to blow the horn: doo—doo—doo!—some kind of beautiful signal. And that will mean: Come out, Smirnov.

The boy is silent for a long time, snuffling and fidgeting on the cracked stool. Then he answers matter-of-factly:

"I will hide."

Oh my goodness, what am I doing, Snetkov wonders to himself in fright, following the boy through the curtains, his hunched, rickety back squeezed into a too-tight plaid jacket with a partly ripped hood.—My God, how slow can he go through the yard, visible to anyone who happens to glance across it; now he's even stopped—stunned by the sudden avalanche of jackdaws from the belfry—he's standing, craning his head, reconsidering; he's not going to climb up the belfry? That's useless, dangerous, no one suggested the belfry, no, some little basement, shed, some inconspicuous hole... Good, he's decided against it, gone on, is going past the belfry, past the cathedral, where, thank God, those two unnecessary witnesses have left the porch for somewhere else. He looks around with a shiver, disappears behind the corner of the cafeteria; and Snetkov now decides to go outside. He does and looks at the clock. There are eighteen minutes left till the end of rest hour.

Back in the days when it was common for the boarding school to be called the forest school, Snetkov called rest hour on the mountain "quiet," and he loved it because he considered it his hour of freedom—while the rest of the day he was irritated. The staff's laziness and stupidity was irritating, the silly quibbles the matrons and teachers had with him when he was still a young doctor were irritating, but more irritating than anything else were the kids: why do they run about as if someone has scalded them, why do they shriek as if they are going to be butchered, why do they scream such absurd, repulsive, even entirely unprintable words at each other? What is the point of hurting, tugging, teasing each other so cruelly, only to cry, only to complain loudly, only to tattle to the no less shrieky and excessively gruff matrons? Where does the sour and oppressive smell come from, as they mob the treatment and examination rooms? They are taken to the *banya*, they are in fact strictly forced to wash their feet and teeth before bed!… During the morning hours when the children sat in class, when their screaming was only heard in the breaks, Snetkov was even more incapable of being alone with himself: frenetically and angrily he scribbled down the required daily notes for the case records, prepared reports and requests for the Regional Health Administration—and those were the most hateful hours of his life. At lunch he ate. In the cafeteria the duraluminum bowls and spoons rattled, mouths munched, the same cries and complaints were heard… But—the trumpet blared, quiet hour came, and the children fell asleep. The teachers went to the city, the matrons dozed off, the doctors and nurses napped on the cold imitation-leather couches in the clinic. He alone kept vigil. He and the mountain.

He would listen to the mountain's talk, which was directed at him alone. For him, a sheet of iron on the cathedral's rusty cupola would suddenly begin to ring quietly and patter; for him, the trees in the coniferous forest would now sigh, now drone, and now cry like wolves; for him, the wind made the waves fizz on the banks down below, near the steep cliff of the mountain; for him, a small steamer whistled far away, a tugboat responded to the steamer; and if it was like it is now—a clear autumn day—and if it happened that at precisely this hour a slow formation of migrating gray birds flew over the mountain, then it would seem to Snetkov that they were parting from him with weary, weeping voices.

His soul softened, his heart lighter, a book in his hand, he would go out the gate and head down the mountain to the river. The mountain's almost vertical limestone cliff towered so high over the water that its ominous quivering shadow, even at that midday hour, would cover the surface of the water to the farthest buoys. Snetkov would sit in the shade, on the trunk of a fallen pine tree bleached by wind and moisture, open his book to the middle and begin to read, rhythmically nodding his head and moving his lips: "...If you act, you will suffer. If you possess something, you will lose it. That is why the wise one is inactive and doesn't suffer failure. He has nothing, and therefore has nothing to lose..." Snetkov would grow blissfully tired, detach himself from the book, lift his head—resting his moist gaze on the peak of the cliff, crowned with the reddish brown underbrush of bushes and a mossy brick wall, the cathedral's cupola just barely peeking out above it. He would think that he was thinking about the Tao—and in his inspired imagination the Tao assumed the features of Lenochka Ts., the eternal student from the Leningrad Academy of Art. Once a month, no more, and always without warning, Lenochka Ts. appeared on the mountain with a bag full of books, and talked about the Tao, about concentrated ying and impetuous yang, about contemptible volition, about nightmarish existence, about chakra, about karma, about flying saucers with extraterrestrial origins, about the surprising gift of some Antonina Mikhailovna from Liteinyi Prospekt, whose bottomless and penetrating look could move her antique furniture from place to place in her prewar apartment. Lenochka always talked with neither pauses nor spaces between her words—an endless stream so long that there was almost no time for him to make love to her afterwards. If Snetkov tried to interrupt her, get a word in edgewise, one that had been diligently prepared since their last meeting, or, even worse, to contradict, she would sincerely, childishly, take offense, and frequently even cry, so Snetkov quickly learned not to interrupt and to remain gratefully silent.

He would patiently listen, make love to her hastily in the clinic, and then she would depart, disappeared for a month or two, leaving him one or two books from her bag… And like this, they passed not one, not two, but three whole years. In the fourth, at the beginning of '79, on the last day of the students' winter break, Lenochka Ts. did not show up alone—but in the company of a skinny, bearded man with wide cheekbones. Greeting him, the bearded man removed his fur *malakhai* and guiltily-triumphantly bowed his head to Snetkov, unveiling a large pink lump that shone through the thinning hair on the very top of his head.

"As you probably realize, this is my husband," Lenochka explained to Snetkov matter-of-factly, and, as it were, annoyed. "So I'm no longer Ts., but P. A most miraculous event, very funny; if I have time, I'll tell you."

The three of them wandered on and around the mountain all afternoon, then they bravely set out across the ice to the opposite bank of the river. Lenochka talked non-stop about Krishna and Buddha, *Kamasutra* and *Domostroi*, while, from under his malakhai, her bearded husband P. winked furtively at Snetkov, as if to say: Let her speak, we'll be patient; and Snetkov winked back unintentionally with his eyes tearing up from the wind… In the middle of the river they halted, turned around all at once and looked at the mountain. It was overcast. The mountain rose up over the ice in a cloud; the cathedral's rusty cupola peeked out of this dark cloud like a dead sun fading. Lenochka said: "Ooh," and stopped talking; her husband asked:

"Have you read *The Magic Mountain,* Snetkov?"

Snetkov had not read *The Magic Mountain.*

"What an oversight, what a terrible oversight," said her husband sternly to Lenochka. "I'll send you *The Magic Mountain* right away, Snetkov; I have it; you'll be stunned by the similarities… There's also a mountain; it's also beautiful; they also have talks about the most important things in life; many implications, Snetkov, are like hovering in the air."

"In the purest air!" piped in Lenochka, making up for her oversight. "And the main thing is—it's really funny—there's also a sanatorium for tuberculosis there…"

"Why not, I'll read it," said Snetkov, embarrassed…

Before saying goodbye, Lenochka asked Snetkov to touch the pink lump on the crown of her husband's head. Snetkov touched it. Said it was nothing dangerous, an ordinary fatty growth that could be cut out or left in peace—depending on what you want. Lenochka asked him to cut it out.

"I'm not a surgeon," said Snetkov. "I don't have anything to do with that."

They went away forever. It was not that Snetkov was upset, but he was irritated. The regular routine of emotion, expectation, and anticipation had been destroyed. Trying to retain faith—not in Lenochka, but in order—he spent his hours of quiet freedom reading about what an individual is and about what an individual perceives himself to be. "…We see," read Snetkov reverently as before, yet moving his lips without the former bliss, "that dueling found its greatest resonance and was practiced with bloodthirsty seriousness in precisely those countries that showed a lack of genuine conscientiousness…" In the spring he sought out a replacement for Lenochka in the city, not just one, but two, although he didn't particularly like being in the city. He forgot about his unfaithful girlfriend and the bearded man, but at the end of autumn the latter reminded Snetkov of his existence by sending a package: two shabby brown volumes from Thomas Mann's collected works. This was *The Magic Mountain.* A note was attached to the package: "Dear Snetkov! As a man of honor, I have kept my word. Excuse me for the delay. Read as much as you like, but then please return them. Yours P. P.S. I decided to keep the lump: what if I suddenly had all my intelligence in it? This, of course, is a joke. P.P.S. It's too bad you aren't a surgeon. Then I'd ask you to cut out the tongue of one of our friends." And Snetkov began *The Magic Mountain.*

The promised similarities were but few. Yes, a mountain, yes, a lung clinic, fresh air, yet not much more than that. Striking, actually, were the dissimilarities, but they didn't hurt: the novel's events took place in a very different country, in a very different, fantastical world, in a different, bygone time. So the magical life in the fictitious sanatorium did not make Snetkov any more envious or astonished than the life in some model human orangery in some ancient utopian or brand-new fantasy novel. It was more that this life aroused a certain feeling of superiority in Snetkov... Yes, there was not and could not be such high-quality food and service on his mountain, and yet, on the magical Swiss mountain there was not—and at that long-past time could not have been—such high-quality treatment. For an enormous amount of money the inhabitants of the Berghof sanatorium deluded themselves with alp cream, individual baths and camelhair blankets so they would think a little less about the powerless doctors and their all-powerful, nearly inevitable death. And yet, his patients at the forest school—forced to sleep in overcrowded public dorms and eat whatever they got out of a communal duraluminum cauldron—could make use of contemporary medicine's achievements at absolutely no cost, and knew no fear. Snetkov scrupulously plowed through both volumes and sent them back to Leningrad with a note: "Dear P.! I am returning *The Magic Mountain* as you requested. I found the novel long-winded and boring. As for the conversations 'about the most important things in life,' about the many implications, which, as you said, 'are hovering in the purest air' of the novel's pages—these conversations and these implications could not protect the world from war or save Hans Castorp from trench dirt. The difficult children in our lives, who have been entrusted to my care, generally curse and smoke, not cigars, but Severok, behind my back, yet their future on the whole does not worry me. Yours, Snetkov."

Only one completely insignificant point in the novel piqued him—the "blood-red" extract from the prickly rose, which an extremely offensive lady drank with commendable persistency... In fact, he had always known, no less so than Thomas Mann, that the berries of the prickly rose (*rosa acicularis*) are exceptionally rich in vitamin C, but to his own embarrassment he'd never once considered that the dense bushes—which grew neglected on the slope of the mountain, which dried up the bodies of the ancient apple trees on the terraces of the former monastery garden, whose malicious roots ate away at the base of the brick wall, whose thorny branches devoured the wall all the way up to its low top—that this unfriendly overgrowth, which housed so many mouse holes, snake nests and children's secrets, was also a prickly rose, rosa acicularis, rich in vitamin C. And from the very minute he read it in Thomas Mann, that useful blood-red extract had not left Snetkov's head. Spring came; the prickly rose—bewildered by the unexpected attention it received—bloomed diligently, promising an unprecedented plethora of medicinal berries with its unprecedented plethora of rose petals. Snetkov impatiently waited for what was promised, and finally the day arrived when he instructed the bugler to blow the horn for a gathering where—not knowing how to put it better—he announced a battle for the harvest. The rose hips they collected lasted a long time; plenty of extract came out of them: now yellow, almost transparent, now rusty-brown, now so black it parched their mouths and was hardly suited for drinking, but whatever the cooks did to conjure up the bloody hue, they failed to achieve it. Snetkov became edgy, irritated, then tired and told himself that the anomalous bright-red drink had been thought up by the author of *The Magic Mountain* as an embellishment. That's why they are writers, to take in credulous minds not particularly concerned with actual reality. In reality there are no magic mountains; nature proffers no alp cream, smooth camel blankets and, definitely, no bloody red drinks... Somewhere there is, as was suddenly noticed, real blood, in a place thousands of miles away where the best boarding-school nurse followed her officer husband. There is dysentery, which her successor brought onto the mountain. In order to cope with the epidemic, Snetkov had to establish a month-long quarantine and poison the mountain air for a long time with caustic disinfectant. There is theft, which was noticed only when the regular weighing of the kids began to produce strange and depressing results. There is, as Snetkov discovered to his astonishment, universal threat to life. Even after the thieves—the administrator, chauffeur and dishwasher—had been exposed, the children's rations did not stop getting skimpier, and, even worse, the medicine began to arrive irregularly. The scenes that Snetkov made with increasing rage in the city and regional public health offices, his humble complaints at the local and central Ministry of Health, all came to nothing. Literally everything around the mountain became skimpy and dilapidated, everything slid inexorably downward, and nothing could stem the slide except nerves and cursing, except invocations and feverish hopes. Snetkov was at a loss. He—likening himself to the wise one—had long since stopped hoping for anything, but suggested all the same that the din of the collapse was still an insufficient and even inappropriate basis for hope… In time, too tempestuous and importunate to brush aside, Snetkov began to think that even the mountain was unstable, that the river's waters were washing away the limestone at its base… This was not speculation in the spirit of the books from Lenochka's bag. This was an ailment akin to dizziness and—his dream almost every night: the mountain splits, the cafeteria sinks into the earth, the empty school caves in, and after it goes the dormitory with its sleeping kids and the cathedral with its collection of tourists from who knows where. He can hear them happily singing, flying into the void, then he can hear soft splashes, one after the other; the spraying water spattering onto the deformed dusty surface; the melancholic pleasure of rescuing people grips Snetkov for an instant, but the belfry shutters, the bell breaks loose and, slowly spinning, flies down, attempting to land right on his head. "Where's the bell coming from? There is no such bell! Why didn't they warn me?" Snetkov wonders before waking up with a languid head and the conviction that he has to stop drinking diluted alcohol at night—it is time to switch to motherwort and valerian… More and more frequently, children arrived on the mountain whom Snetkov later found to have gastric, nephritic or other chronic afflictions having nothing to do with the mountain. More and more infrequently did the regional hospital agree to admit these children for treatment: it examined them, specified the diagnosis and, making reference to the shortage of space and the waiting list, sent them back to the mountain or to their parents… A young girl who was brought to the mountain one day from the Voskhod settlement had to be taken to intensive care on the third day during a terrible asthma attack. The young girl survived the long, persistent, almost deadly suffocation with hardly any fear—with such composure and resignation that there could hardly be any doubt about her extensive experience. Snetkov could not believe that the Voskhod doctors contrived to overlook her asthma. He reviewed the pages in the standard case record—one and all signed with an indecipherable, faded flourish similar to a slug—and determined that fourteen pages were missing. Such an indecipherable flourish simply fused a very sick child to a mountain that was not designed for serious illnesses and—so she was sure to be admitted—they took any mention of asthma out of the accompanying pages…

"Certainly it's barbarous!" they said compassionately to Snetkov at the regional office of health. "Criminal barbarity, but it's understandable. Zoya Malukova, nine years old, judging by everything, is very ill and will be ill for a long time. Though you can put her in a hospital, you can't stay in a hospital your whole life, you also have to go back home at some point, and put yourself at the mercy of the Voskhod doctors. But Voskhod, Snetkov—think about it—it's on the Moon. You managed to bring Zoya Malukova to intensive care, but the one who signs with a flourish (we know this flourish: not a bad guy, even if he's crap)—he probably wouldn't have… But why are we speaking of Voskhod, Snetkov! All of us are on the Moon: no medicine, no room for patients, not even a rudimentary conscience. At least you've got food… Of course they're foisted on you. And they'll continue to be foisted on you, get used to it."

After this strange conversation Snetkov drank a glass of cognac at a students' café in the city and headed back to the mountain in a daze—even forgetting to visit his girls… On the bus a baby screamed nastily; its mother, calming it, screamed nastily. On the mountain it was quiet hour. "Essentially, all of them have been foisted on us," thought Snetkov distractedly. "I, essentially, can improve their health, but I can't improve their lives. I'm not a nanny, I can't even talk with them"… "Rest hour," he recalled; it lodged in his heart, and since then he has not enjoyed this hour, has been afraid to remain alone with himself, not knowing any outlet for his lonely alarmed soul until the kids come alive, until they start to shout, scream, scramble, until they fling the oppressive, meaningless silence off the mountain.

---

Page 94, *Malakhai:* A cap with large earflaps.
Page 94, *Domostroi*: A handbook on religion, morality, and household management; it stressed the importance of hierarchy and stability in the Russian family. It is thought to have been published during the 1550s; the author is unknown.
Page 96, *Severok*: A brand of cigarettes in the Soviet Union.
Page 97, *Somewhere there is…her officer husband*: This passage is a reference to the beginning of the Soviet invasion of Afghanistan in December 1979.

# Three Poems by Itoh Masako

Translated by Eric Selland from Japanese (Japan)

Little is known about Itoh Masako except that she was married briefly to the well-known anti-war poet Ayukawa Nobuo and then died of illness during WWII. She was a member, along with Ayukawa, of the *Shin-Ryodo* (New Country) group, which remained actively involved in leftist and various social concerns throughout the 1930s, even after the instigation of draconian laws by the Japanese Fascists keeping tight control over all aspects of public and private life, especially creative expression including publishing.

Itoh is known to have published two books in her lifetime, *Shin-Shishū* (New Poems) in 1934 and *Maya Oyomesan to Inu* (Maya the Bride and Her Dog), but no copies of these publications are known to be in existence. Itoh is one of a group of women experimental poets associated with the magazine *Madame Blanche* where these poems were originally published. It was an outgrowth of the avant-garde poet Kitasono Katue's *VOU* group, which was especially open to women writers. Most of these women also published in the major Modernist magazine *Shi to Shiron* (Poetry and Poetics) originally inaugurated by Nishiwaki Junzaburo—the Ezra Pound of Japan.

Itoh's Surrealist influence is evident here, and some of the poems seem to hint at the beginnings of a shift in interest towards realism and social concerns. One of the interesting elements in the work of the *Madame Blanche* poets is the beginnings of what would later become the women's poetry of the postwar period, which weaves social and political concerns as well as a new Feminist awareness into poems that focus on the daily lives of women.

A Modernist tendency can be seen on a number of levels in these poems. For instance the frequent use of foreign words such as "souvenir," or "Traviata," likely referring to the heroine of the Verdi opera, written in katakana, the angular syllabary used to write foreign words and which at the time was used in telexes and advertisements. Foreign words and places in the poem would have been both exotic and modern, as well as somewhat jolting for the reader more accustomed to traditional poetic language and forms. But then Itoh softens the mood by using the hiragana syllabary, the more feminine, cursive form associated with the classics and women's writing in particular, in cases where the conventional approach would be to use a kanji character. These graphic or visual elements, which are of course lost in translation, were important innovative elements of the experimental poetry of the time.

Even the choice of a common word such as "street" in the title of one of the poems here points to the Modernist and innovative nature of Itoh's poetry. The word in Japanese, *douro*, is a decidedly unromantic, unpoetic term referring literally to the broad asphalt thoroughfares of the modern metropolis, an image which would have had no place in Japanese poetry for the generation previous to Itoh's.

Itoh Masako's work was forgotten, along with that of the other *Madame Blanche* poets, in the course of a violent and discontinuous history, as well as the vagaries of the process of literary canonization during the postwar period. The work of the Japanese interwar experimental women poets is still for the most part unknown even in Japan, but there are a growing number of scholars and poets who have taken interest, and the process of recovering their work has begun.

Original text: Itoh Masako, "Te no rekishi," "Subeniiru," and "Douro," from *Madame Blanche*.

# 手の歴史

しばらく　　　　やさしさも消えて
物語のなかの日曜日
暖毛套をゆすぶり　　　　終日
賑やかな編飾を編みほぐす
海邊の歴史について　　青白い壁書について
緑色の群集について
髭のない音楽家たちよ
ヂキタリスの花についてもう一度語ろうではないか
数々の手が集まり火花を散らして
うらぶれた一頁を開けば
もう一本の絃も切れてしまった

# History of the Hand

For a time  even gentleness disappeared
A storybook Sunday
My warm, plush earmuffs hang loosely  all day long
Flourishing ornaments are knitted and then disentangled
About the history of the seashore  and the ghastly legal notices posted on walls
And about the green community
Oh beardless musicians
Let us speak again of foxglove flowers
Gathering the many hands and scattering sparks
Opening the book to a ragged page
Another violin string snaps

# スヴェニイル

昨日失われるまで
花のないひびきにゆれながら
それはとほい湖水にまき散らされた月桂樹であろう
ナザレの丘になほもめぐる人魚の黒潮をのこして
憂はしげなるトラヴィアタよ
天使らの生誕にもまして美はしいそなたらの天稟はふたたび白い馬上へとおくりかへされるのでもあったろうか

# Souvenir

Till it vanished yesterday
Swaying in an echo without flowers
It is laurel strewn over a faraway lake
Leaving behind the black current of the mermaids still circling the Nazareth Hills
Oh melancholy Traviata
Were your gifts, all the more elegant at the birth of the angels, sent back perhaps,
placed once again on the backs of white horses?

# 道路

縞々のかげもある
とっておきの思い出なら
クの字型に
鴉の子も啼きませうに

# Street

There are shadows of stripes also
A treasured memory—
Should not the children of the crow cry also
In the shape of an alternate alphabet

# Doxa

Marcel Cohen | Translated by Raphael Rubinstein from French (France)

"Doxa," a prose text written in French by Marcel Cohen, takes as its subject a wristwatch that belonged to the poet Paul Celan. It was first published in a limited edition in 2008 by Editions de l'Attente in Bordeaux, France. Like all of Cohen's writings, "Doxa" (the name of the Swiss company that made the watch) is economical, restrained, precise, and harrowing. Moving backwards in time from the day of Celan's 1970 suicide, it embarks on an almost forensic examination of the poet's most treasured possession, along the way constructing a micro-biography that draws on technical watchmakers' terminology.

Marcel Cohen was born in the Paris suburb of Asnières in 1937. Since his debut novel in 1969, he has published numerous volumes made up of short narratives. Several of his books have been translated into English, including *Mirrors*, *The Emperor Peacock Moth*, and *Walls*. In the U.S. he is perhaps best known for his volume of interviews with Edmond Jabès, published in English as *From the Desert to the Book*.

In 2005, Ibis Editions published my translation of his book *In Search of a Lost Ladino: Letter to Antonio Saura*, a meditation on the vanished Sephardic culture of the Ottoman Empire and Cohen's own relationship to the Judeo-Spanish language of his childhood. In my introduction to *In Search of a Lost Ladino* I describe how this text presents unusual challenges to its translator. It was originally written in Judeo-Spanish (or Ladino), a language the author knew from his youth but had never written in before. He subsequently translated this text into French; my version is based on the French version, but also takes into account the Ladino original.

In his complex diasporic linguistic identity Cohen has obvious affinities with Celan, who wrote fluently in Romanian, German, and French, each language carrying a different symbolic weight. Like Celan, Cohen suffered irreparable losses in the Holocaust: this is one of the subtexts of "Doxa." Cohen examines this battered, talismanic timepiece for clues to the poet's life and death. In recent decades, Celan has been the subject of more commentary than perhaps any other 20th-century poet. In "Doxa," Cohen reaffirms the obdurate reality that underlies Celan's work.

Original text: Marcel Cohen, *Doxa*. Bordeaux: Editions de l'Attente, 2008.

# Doxa

Dans la nuit du 19 au 20 avril 1970, le poète Paul Celan ôte sa montre-bracelet, la pose en évidence sur un meuble, au troisième étage du 6 avenue Emile Zola et va se jeter dans la Seine du Pont Mirabeau, à quelques dizaines de mètres de son domicile.

Avec un exemplaire relié en cuir bleu du *Faust* de Goethe, publié aux Editions Insel de Leipzig, et offert par des amis de la famille, cette montre est tout ce que Paul Celan avait pu préserver de son enfance à Czernowitz, en Bucovine, ancienne province autrichienne devenue roumaine en 1918. La montre lui avait été offerte par ses parents en 1933, l'année de ses treize ans, pour sa bar-mitsva.

Déportés en 1942, les parents de Paul Celan mourront dans les camps, successivement roumains puis allemands : son père est victime du typhus, sa mère, apprendra-t-il, aurait été exécutée d'une balle dans la nuque. Paul Celan lui-même passera deux ans dans les camps de travail de Moldavie.

En acier inoxydable, rectangulaire et de forme curvexe, la montre porte la marque *Doxa* («opinion» en grec, mais aussi «gloire») et l'indication «antimagnétique». Le bracelet en box noir est trop étroit pour le boîtier, si bien que la montre flotte un peu sur ses deux fixations, les «pompes» en termes d'horlogerie. Le cuir est fortement marqué par la boucle et l'ardillon. Depuis longtemps déjà, ce bracelet méritait donc d'être remplacé.

Le cadran noir de la *Doxa* est pourvu, à six heures, d'une petite fenêtre carrée pour la trotteuse des secondes. Il est fêlé ainsi que le verre. L'aiguille des heures et celle des minutes sont en forme de glaive, une forme courante dans les années trente …

# Doxa

During the night of April 19-20, 1970, the poet Paul Celan took off his wristwatch, placed it conspicuously on a piece of furniture on the fourth floor of 6 Avenue Emile Zola and went out to jump into the Seine from the Pont Mirabeau, a few dozen meters from his home.

Along with a copy of Goethe's *Faust*, bound in blue leather, published by Editions Insel of Leipzig and given to him by family friends, this watch is all that Paul Celan was able to save from his childhood in Czernowitz, Bukovina, the former Austrian province that became part of Romania in 1918. His parents gave him the watch in 1933, when he was 13, as a bar mitzvah present.

Deported in 1942, Paul Celan's parents died in the camps, Romanian and German: his father fell victim to typhus; his mother, he would learn, had been executed with a bullet to the neck. Paul Celan himself spent two years in labor camps in Moldavia.

Made of stainless steel, rectangular and curvex in form, the watch carries the trademark Doxa ("opinion" in Greek, but also "glory") and the indication "antimagnétique." The black box-leather band is too narrow for the case, so much so that the watch floats a little on its two pins, the *pompes* in watchmaker's terms. The leather is strongly marked by the buckle and tongue. For a long time, this band has needed replacing.

The black face of the Doxa features a small square window, at six o'clock, for the second hand. The face is cracked, as is the glass. The hour and minute hands are shaped like swords, a common design in the 1930s; however, only the minute hand is phosphorescent. Thus, the shorter hand isn't original.

No watchmaker would replace an hour hand without

also proposing to change a damaged watch face. From this we can deduce either that the watchmaker wasn't able to procure a new watch face or that Paul Celan didn't want to have the old one replaced. After an impact violent enough to break the face and hand, the glass wouldn't have been simply cracked, as it is today. It would have had to be replaced at the same time as the hour hand.

The new hour hand is made of black tempered steel. As with most watches, this is a standard part that varies only in its finish, depending on the make and model. In this case, while the form of the new hour hand corresponds to the shape of the original minute hand, its raw metal, lacking any chrome, enamel, or phosphorescent coating, does considerable aesthetic harm to the watch. A watchmaker would only have installed this new hour hand if called on to make an emergency repair. How could such a repair not convey a sense of penury?

While not rich, Paul Celan's parents didn't want for anything: a commercial agent, his father worked in the lumber industry. For an occasion as solemn as the bar mitzvah of their only child they would never have given a shoddy wristwatch. Besides, the longevity of the watch proves the robustness of the movements purveyed by Doxa, a small firm operating in the Jura region of Switzerland since 1889. That the watch was of Swiss manufacture guaranteed the future availability of replacement parts.

The impossibility of finding an hour hand conforming to the minute hand and also, possibly, a face, indicates that, in all likelihood, the repairs were made immediately after the war. Whether they were done in Bucharest, where Paul Celan lived from 1945 to 1947, in Austria where he spent several months after having escaped from Romania, in France where he permanently established himself or, all the more so, in a Germany rising from the ruins where his work was published from 1949 on, only reinforces the presumption of a scarcity of watch parts—parts that, in any case, would have been extremely costly, like everything that was imported from Switzerland during this period.

If the cracks one sees today in the glass of the Doxa are not contemporary with the impact that made the replacement of the hour hand necessary, was the glass broken a second time? If so, why didn't Paul Celan change it? Was the glass broken in the months, weeks or days preceding the night of April 19-20? Did Celan see no point in getting his watch fixed?

In the course of decades, the crown of the Doxa lost all its chrome coating. Denuded, the yellow brass cuts into the stainless steel of the case in a disgraceful manner. Yet, this crown could easily have been replaced. The crown on a typical watch is a standard element, just like the hands, the face and the glass (only the five Swiss "fabriques" specializing in luxury watches produce all the parts needed for their models, apart from the spring). If, extraordinarily, this part was no longer available in Switzerland—even though the Doxa company, based in Le Locle since it was founded, continues to exist—nothing could have prevented the crown from being dipped into a bath of chrome: an affordable repair and, in any case, incomparable to the sentimental value that Paul Celan attached to this watch. Numerous photographs confirm that the Doxa never left his wrist.

Again one must pose a question: Did Paul Celan ever consider having the crown repaired? Clues as blinding as this worn-out crown, broken face, cracked glass and mismatched hour hand—was their function, for a man so lucid and attentive about dates, to enable him to embrace in a single glance, everywhere and under any circumstances, the present moment and the disasters of the past, pointing to the only time that, in his eyes, was always accurate?

*The author warmly thanks Eric Celan and Bertrand Badiou.*

# Two Poems by Kabir

Translated by Arvind Krishna Mehrotra from Hindi (India)

About Kabir few facts are certain. According to some legends he was born in 1398 and died in 1518, though others, more realistically, give him a shorter life span. In one birth legend, a Brahmin widow accompanied her father to the shrine of a famous ascetic. Pleased with her devotion, the ascetic prayed that she be blessed with a son. The prayer was answered, and in due course a son was born to her. But there was one problem: Brahmin widows are not supposed to get pregnant, and she had to abandon the infant. The wife of a weaver, who was passing that way, discovered the child and took him home. The child was Kabir.

Weavers in India have traditionally been Muslim and there is reason to believe that Kabir was also, due to scattered references to weaving in his poems. Though a few thousand poems are ascribed to Kabir, we cannot be certain of the authorship of even one. And to make textual matters worse, these poems come in several versions. Luc Sante has said of the blues that they are examples of "collective creation"; the lines of the song could be "altered, extended, abridged, and transposed" by the singer, if they so wished. The same is true of a Kabir poem.

Kabir belonged to the popular devotional movement called *bhakti*. The word is derived from the Sanskrit root *bhaj*, and one of its meanings is "to serve, honor, revere, love, adore." The *bhakta*, the "devotee" or "lover of God," looks upon God with a certain intimacy. The focus is on inward love for the One Deity, without regard to Brahminical ritual. It is no surprise therefore that many of the great bhakti poets, who were at the vanguard of this movement, came from the bottom of the Hindu caste ladder. The poet-saint was often a cobbler, tailor, barber, or weaver.

Kabir has had many translators, including scholars and poets, and my translations fall somewhere between the scholarly and the poetic. Unlike Rabindranath Tagore and Robert Bly, two of the best-known poet-translators of Kabir, I have closely read the originals; but unlike the scholars (Charlotte Vaudeville, Linda Hess), I don't feel bound to strictly translate every word. Like the blues singer, I too have "altered, extended, abridged, and transposed," all the while keeping the original and the commentaries in mind.

Original text: Kabir, "Running up minarets..." and "When greed hits you like a wave..." from *Kabir Granthavali*, ed. Parasnath Tiwari. Allahabad: Hindi Parishad, 1961.

कहु रे मुल्ला बांग निवाजा ।
एक मसीति दसौं दरवाजा ।। टेक ।।
मनु करि मका किबला करि देही । बोलनहारु परम गुर एही ।।१।।
बिसिमिलि तांमसु भरमु कंदूरी । भखि लै पंचैं होइ सबूरी ।।२।।
कहै कबीर मैं भया दिवांनां । मुसि मुसि मनुवां सहजि समांनां ।।३।।

Running up minarets,
Calling out to the faithful
Five times a day,
What's your problem, muezzin?

Can't you see you're a walking
Mosque yourself?
Your mind's your Mecca;
Your body the Ka'aba
That you face when you pray;
Anything you say
Is an utterance from heaven.
Cut the throat of desire,
Not of a poor goat, if you must.

I'm as one possessed, says Kabir.
Only don't ask me how
It all happened, or when.

जियरा जाहुगे हंम जांनीं ।
आवैगी कोई लहरि लोभ की बूड़ैगा बिनू पांनीं ॥ टेक ॥
राज करंता राजा जाइगा रूप दिपंती रांनीं ।
जोग करंता जोगी जाइगा कथा सुनंता ग्यांनीं ॥ १ ॥
चंद जाइगा सूर जाइगा जाइगा पवन औ पांनीं ।
कहै कबीर तेरा संत न जाइगा रांम भगति ठहरांनीं ॥ २ ॥

When greed hits you like a wave
You don't need water to drown.

Whether it's reigning king
Or pretty queen,

Chanting pundit
Or miracle-working yogi,

They'll die by drowning
In a waterless sea.

Who survives? Those, says Kabir,
Whose minds are tied to rocks

# Two Translators on Gennady Aygi

Peter France and Sarah Valentine

Gennady Aygi (1934-2006) was the national poet of Chuvashia, a Turkic-speaking republic within the Russian Federation, some 450 miles east of Moscow. In Russian, and through translation into many languages, he was also recognized as one of the outstanding Russian-language poets of the later twentieth-century, a pioneering writer of free verse who left a monumental body of work. He was several times nominated for the Nobel Prize for literature.

PETER FRANCE

# Poetry and Prose by Gennady Aygi

Translated by Peter France from Russian (Chuvashia)

I was a close friend of Gennady Aygi's from our first meeting in 1974, and have translated several volumes of his poetry into English; in particular *Selected Poems, 1954–1994*, *Salute—to Singing*, *Child-and-Rose*, *Field-Russia* and *Winter Revels*. Aygi is not an easy poet —for some Russian readers he is too "hermetic"— and I first began to translate him as a kind of conversation with the author (from whom I was separated by the Iron Curtain), and as a way of coming to a closer understanding of poems whose importance was already clear to me.

Having translated so much of his verse, together with some aphoristic writings on poetry, I have, since his death, been working on the prose writings in which he pays tribute to some of the writers who meant most to him; interspersed with some verse tributes such as "Requiem before Winter" (a poem in memory of his "second father," Boris Pasternak, whom he knew well at the end of the older poet's life); these will be published by New Directions under the title *Time of Gratitude*. Gratitude is indeed a recurrent theme of his writing, gratitude to the natural world and its creator, but also gratitude to many men and women, especially poets, artists and musicians. These figures, both the great dead and living contemporaries, were particularly important as a source of strength and inspiration for a village boy living in Moscow in the oppressive Brezhnev years, when Aygi survived in an artistic underground, virtually unpublished in the USSR.

The subjects of these tributes include some of the great Russian writers and artists of the twentieth century, Pasternak, Khlebnikov, Mayakovsky, Malevich, Shalamov, but also some key figures in European modernism, from Baudelaire and Norwid to Celan and Char. Franz Kafka, the subject of the present text, became known to Aygi through French translations in 1961, and this discovery transformed him. To the end of his life, Kafka was like a literary "saint" for him, figuring not only in this tribute, but in a whole series of poems. To use an expression dear to Aygi, Kafka was a source of light.

PETER FRANCE

Original text: Gennady Aygi, *Razgovor na rasstoyanii.* St Petersburg: Limbus Press, 2001.

# ПРЕДЗИМНИЙ РЕКВИЕМ

*Памяти Б. Л. Пастернака*

провожу и останусь как хор молчаливый
я в божьем пространстве весь день предуказанный
с движеньями зимнего четкого дня
словно с сажею рядом

а время творится само по себе
кружится пущенный по миру снег
у монастырских ворот
и кажется ныне поддержкой извне
необходимость прохожих

а уровень века уже утвержден
и требует уровень славы
лицо к тишине обращать
и не книга но атлас страстей
в тиши на столе сохранен

# Requiem Before Winter

## *In memory of Boris Pasternak*

I shall follow and remain like a silent choir
in the space of god all the preordained day
alongside the shifts of the clear winter day
as alongside soot

but time is of itself self-created
hurled into the world snow whirls
round the monastery gates
and the inevitable passers-by
seem now a support from without

but the level of the century is already fixed
and the level of fame demands
that the face be turned toward quietness
and not a book but an atlas of passions
is preserved in quiet on the desk

а год словно сажа коснется домов
в веке старом где будто разорваны книги
и любая страница потребует
линий резки и складки к себе
через мои рукава
где холод где рядом окно а за ним
сугробы ворота дома

but like soot the year will touch the houses
in the old century where books seem torn up
and any of the pages will demand
lines of cutting and folding inward
across my sleeves
with the cold and the window nearby and outside
the snowdrifts the gates the houses

# О ДА: СВЕТ КАФКИ

Летом прошлого года моя сестра ездила в Прагу. Я попросил ее посетить старое пражское кладбище и положить от моего имени “московский” камушек на могилу Кафки (я знал, что так делали когда-то евреи при посещении дорогих им могил).

На другой день после того как сестра выполнила мое обещание, ее захотела увидеть одна пражская женщина. Слово “шок”, - я никогда не произносил его по отношению к себе. Но я испытал именно это состояние, когда узнал, кем была эта женщина.

«Дочь - Оттлы? - повторил я, - дочь - Оттлы? Разве это возможно?»

Кафка, его сестры, Освенцим, мужья его сестер, пепел, почти все его родственники, фотография Кафки перед глазами - с его любимой сестрой, пепел и освенцимский дым, и вдруг - в свете московского дня, просто - «дочь Оттлы?» - и слова сестры: «Она знает твое имя и кланяется тебе».

Придя в себя, я сказал: «У меня такое чувство, будто я коснулся рукава святого».

В ящике моего письменного стола лежат листья каштана с его могилы и белый камушек - оттуда же... - очень редко я позволяю себе притронуться к ним.

И я осмеливаюсь прикоснуться к святому для меня имени Кафки (я не могу иначе выразиться), хочу сказать о нем кое-что лишь потому, что в моих ушах звучат слова его племянницы: «Я знаю все статьи, опубликованные у вас о моем дяде, но я не знаю, как относятся к нему его обычные читатели»....

# From *O Yes: Light of Kafka*

Last summer my sister went to Prague. I asked her to visit the old cemetery of the city and to lay a "Moscow" stone on Kafka's grave for me (I knew this was what Jews used to do when visiting graves that were dear to them).

The day after my sister carried out my request, a Prague lady expressed a desire to meet her. The word "shock" is one I have never used in relation to myself. But this was exactly what I felt when I found out *who* this woman was.

"The daughter of...Ottla?" I kept repeating, "The daughter...of Ottla? Is it possible?"

Kafka, his sisters, Auschwitz, his sisters' husbands, ash, almost all of his family, a photograph of Kafka before my eyes with his beloved sister, ash and the smoke of Auschwitz, and suddenly, in the light of a Moscow day, this simple "the daughter of Ottla?"—and my sister's words: "She knows your name and she sends you her regards."

Once I had recovered, I said: "I feel as if I have touched the sleeve of a saint."

In my desk drawer there is a chestnut leaf from *his* grave and a white stone—*from the same place* ...—it is only very rarely that I allow myself to touch them.

And now I am venturing to touch the name of Kafka, which is sacred to me (I can find no other way of saying it), I want to say something about him simply because I can hear these words of his niece: "I know all the articles that have been published about my uncle in your country, but I don't know how ordinary readers feel about him."

✤

I know people whose faces shine with a certain expression,

a certain *wordless purity*, and I know how that expression is fully tried and tested—in the world of Kafka's visions.

Such people recognize one another by this strange "Kafka-like" luminosity of the face, just as one believer recognizes, *senses,* another believer.

I am not claiming to be one of these people—not to that degree. I simply want to say that there are such readers of Kafka in Russia.

But one must also mention another type of reader. "How terrible!" is a quite understandable reaction. But "How gloomy!"—how often I have also heard that reaction to Kafka's work (and in all our literary criticism I know only one article which does not degrade his character or seek out "failings" in his work).

There is another common approach to Kafka that could be called the search for "truth in a can."

A goner in a prison camp picks up an empty can on the perimeter and scrapes around in it for the tiniest scrap of something to eat—whence the expression I have just used (it was given me by a now deceased Russian priest).

There are readers who seem almost to take pleasure in searching in Kafka for crumbs of a "truth" in the form of "hints," whereas in Kafka there is the beginning of an almost trans-existential "space"; is there not beyond his "existential" torment the gleam of something whole—not fragmented simply so that "people can understand it"—and does not this unfragmented whole confront us invisibly, concentrating all our attention, our secret being, in an extreme tension, a responsible wholeness, as if we were looking into *something* into which, as we well know, one cannot look?

Kafka is beyond Allegory, beyond Symbol, these gates of the universal human Temple have already closed behind him, he is "somewhere," in an invisible Concentration that is unconcealed yet inaccessible—but even so we seem-to-see-and-hear Him.

We say "the Apophatic"—from the impossibility of speaking—but does it consist simply of *darkness*? And we seem to hear something like an inexpressibly-painful human refrain (about "those who sing in the heavens"): *light*, how then did you come to be—*displaced*?...—how did you—in your oneness—become hidden from souls (of light-and-of-darkness)—together with the darkness?

✤

Once I was very surprised by Akhmatova (who is usually so clear-sighted)—by a line of hers spoken on the radio (the "voice" of somewhere): "Such a thing Kafka might have invented."

But Kafka *invented* nothing, he *saw*.

And what people see is not darkness; with inner human light they see another *Inner Light*.

*Even* Auschwitz does not consist only of darkness (*even such a thing* we cannot imagine otherwise): there is a cry of *light* (invisible, "unheard-of"—yes, we ask: was the Apophatic not split open—in some "mystical time"—in some kind of "repetition"?—we do not know these "times," we know our own time, when Some-Thing-like-that has indeed been split open). Were there ever such *scorched* faces? Is radiation (God forgive me) not a pitiful caricature (something second-hand, third-hand) of the splitting open in time of the Times?

But it is extremely difficult for us to "determine" (and if we "guess at" something, it is impossible to speak it) What or Who is concerned by this *light*...—undoubtedly the light of the Terrible, only not in "our sense," but the Terrible-in-Itself, as in the torments of the Unrevealed-at-a-time-of-Necessary-Revelation. But who, however "knowledgeable" they may be, can affirm that Creation is already complete?—are we not situated *within* some *tragic* stage of its continuation?

A baby is pure (there are depths beyond the reach of "classic Freudianism" or any of its variants), its purity perceives a great deal that is inaccessible to us; and does not this *innocent wisdom*, this *holy wisdom* perceive the *inner light* of the world in a way that cannot be communicated to us in our common language, whereas it is possible to talk with us *in such a way* that within this conversation, inseparable from it, is the terrifying shining of the inexpressible, and we can at least *feel* that?

✤

And this K. is moving among us (he is not only the

hero of two novels—this branding-letter could replace the characters' names in a whole series of Kafka stories), he is wandering, K....—a strange figure no doubt, but in what way?

He would be less than the "living," if we were keeping awake in the name of the familiar slogan: "one has to live"(but why this "has to"?), if we were such "full-blooded people," it would be better to keep away from us.

He is also less than the "full-blooded" figures from the novels of the nineteenth century (or rather of previous centuries), but we are not genuinely awake, we cannot wake into Vigilance-Life, and he wanders among us, this K., who is bigger—and more real—than we are.

And he moves on—in that illumination whose name is the Vigilance of the tormented perspicacity of Kafka; isn't the word "life" sometimes the tautological equivalent of the idea of a *herd mentality*?—and Kafka's "parables" are like an indirect light at a distance from this amorphous fog; but if we achieve wakefulness in blazingly-pitiless Concentration of Day, then any of Kafka's "parables" can occupy the central point of this Concentration; and what is more, we do not dwell so dimly in a drowsy absence of spiritual attention, even that very absence is now like the sky-glow of an all-human alarm ("not-ness" is a particular light) and in it, not as a shadow, but as a distant, irrevocable deep sky-glow, sliding and flickering, wanders K.

# A Few Notes on Poetry

Gennady Aygi | Translated by Sarah Valentine from Russian (Chuvashia)

Most of Gennady Aygi's meditations on poetry, creativity, and the work of his contemporaries take the form of the "lyric essay." They are prose works, to be sure, but are suffused with a poetic approach to language and meaning, evoking the dream-like world of his poems. Such essays are not only thought-provoking and provide great insight into Aygi's concept of poetry and his poetic process, they are aesthetically, rhythmically-driven works in their own right, and can be read as much for their musicality and poetic qualities as for the ideas they express.

"A Few Notes about Poetry" is a meditation on the tasks and characteristics of contemporary poetry "in its pan-European sense." The phrase is significant because Aygi, writing in both Russian and Chuvash, constantly strove to integrate the philosophies of his native culture—reverence for nature, the individual's connection to humanity—with those of the larger Russian and European traditions in which his work was read.

At first glance the essay may seem didactic, a poet's list of dos and don'ts. But I read it more as a conversation the poet is having with himself based on the initial, earnest question: "What should poetry do?" What follows is a series of possibilities that seek to balance various polemic impulses often found in contemporary poetry with a grounding in ancient ethical and spiritual traditions. Both Russian Orthodox Christianity and Chuvash pre-Christian beliefs were important for Aygi and formed the foundation of his aesthetic.

The central question in this piece is important for historical reasons, too. The year 1978 fell in the thick of Brezhnev's infamous "stagnation," a period of political regression and decline in social morale. Conflicts were flaring in the Caucasus region, and within a year the Soviet Union would invade Afghanistan to begin a long, costly, and ultimately futile war. As during Stalinist times, dissident writers and intellectuals were being exiled to the Gulag and other Soviet labor camps. Indeed, for poets it was a time of solemn reflection on creativity, its socio-political role and its consequences.

SARAH VALENTINE

Original text: Gennady Aygi, *Razgovor na rasstoyanii: kniga-al'bom: stat'i, esse, besedy, stikhi*, ed. Viktor Kulle. St. Petersburg: Limbus Press, 2001.

# Несколько абзацев о поэзии

Что делать поэзии (понимаемой, в данном случае, в ее общеевропейском единстве)?

Не сетовать на свои “положения”, подумать о своем поведении.

Наконец, подумать о достоинстве поэтического Слова... А оно—*иоанническое* (определение Слова апостолом продолжает быть действенным: “вот сейчас”, ежесекундно).

(Ответственность и существенность нашего слова—в *метафорическом соответствии.*)

Эти фразы не дня и не года. И теперь нечего сказать, если этого не сказать.

Не частотность “высоких слов”, а *ориентация* на человека в его сопряженности с природой, — с ее неотменимой *чудесностью*.

# A Few Notes on Poetry

What should poetry do (understood, in this context, in its pan-European sense)?

Not complain about its "condition" or think about its behavior.

In the end it should think about the worthiness of the poetic Word... and it is *Ioannian* (the definition of the Word of the apostle still holds: "right now," every second).

(The responsibility and essence of our word is in its *metaphorical accordance.*)

These are not the sayings of the day or year. At this point there is nothing more to say if you don't say that.

Not the frequency of "lofty words" but an *orientation* towards the human in his or her connection with nature—with its unchanging *miraculousness*.

To believe in *simplicity* is the foundation.

Верить в эту *простоту*, как в основу.

Не мимикрировать, чтоб “выжыть”, облекаясь в чуждые для поэзии “языки” (сенсаций, “новостей дня”, экстремистской “за-ангажированности”).

Не эпатировать *бедных*.

Не спекулировать на “отчаянии”. (В подлинном отчаянии, искусство почти бессловесно...—ибо такой уже выжымается *свет*.)

Не только верить, но и свидетельствовать собой, что человек *не оторван* от природы.

“Отчуждение человека от человека”. Не должно быть “законом” то, что должно быть преодолено.

Not to mimic in order to "suffer," dressing up in "languages" that are alien to poetry (sensationalism, the "news of the day," extremist "causes").

Not to shock the *unfortunate*.

Not to speculate on "despair." (In real despair, art is nearly wordless...—for such is the *light* that squeezes through.)

Not only to believe, but to witness itself that man *has not been torn away* from nature.

"The estrangement of man from man." What should be overcome should not be considered "law."

# Tongue

Ibrahim al-Koni | Translated by Elliott Colla from Arabic (Libya)

Nearly a century ago, Max Weber described modernity as "the disenchantment of the world." Apparently the message was never delivered to Ibrahim al-Koni. Born in 1948 into the Kel Ajjer (Twareg) of southern Libya, al-Koni did not learn Arabic until the age of twelve. A few years later, al-Koni was sent to the Soviet Union to study at the Maxim Gorky Literature Institute. After working as a journalist in Moscow and Warsaw for many years, al-Koni finally turned to writing fiction. Though his first language is Tamahaq, al-Koni writes mainly in Arabic, and since the 1970s he has published dozens of novels, short-story collections, as well as books of aphorisms, critical studies and cultural histories. For his accomplishments, he is regarded as one of the most inventive and enigmatic writers of the contemporary Arab world.

Al-Koni is *sui generis*, most at home treating stark themes from Twareg life in the desert—a nomadic environment marked by intense scarcity, reliance on one's self and one's mount, and the persistence of human slavery. Because these are also the themes of the oldest, pre-Islamic works of Arabic literature, the *Mu'allaqat* (or "hanging poems"), al-Koni has been praised for his classicism. Al-Koni's language is similarly classical. Yet his mannered, lyrical style can only be accomplished by someone, like al-Koni, who chooses to write in something other than his mother tongue. At the same time, al-Koni is a promiscuous reader, and his is an eclectic library of citations. Throughout his works, one encounters reworkings of Twareg folklore, *Moby Dick,* and *Gilgamesh,* alongside references to Russian realism, medieval Sufism, or the postmodern Latin American novel.

For the past three years, I've been working on translations of two of al-Koni's novels, *al-Tibr* (published as *Gold Dust*, 2008, runner-up for the 2009 Saif Ghobash-Banipal Translation Prize), and *al-Majus* (forthcoming as *The Animists*, 2010). I was originally drawn to al-Koni for two reasons: his insistence on telling a compelling story; and his rarified language. This last aspect is perhaps why his prose renders so easily into English—it's as if al-Koni's language is not embedded in contemporary Arabic but rather hovers over it as a study.

While working on *al-Majus*, an epic of more than six hundred pages, I needed a distraction and discovered *Kharif al-darwish* (Autumn of the Dervish), a collection of short stories from roughly the same period of the author's career. The stories of this collection present the harrowing scenarios of al-Koni's encyclopedic novels—the fragility of life in the deep desert and the haunted character of the world itself—in a concentrated form. Many of the stories in this collection focus on those organs of the body—eyes, ears, and tongues—where human power and frailty, dignity and violation intersect. "Tongue" is a distilled example of al-Koni's writing style and, in particular, shows off his abilities to set a scene.

Original text: Ibrahim al-Koni, *Kharif al-darwish.* Beirut: Al-Mu'assasat al-'Arabiyya li-l-Dirasat wa-l-Nashr, 1994).

# اللسان

اعتاد النبيل أن يجالس عبده كلما عاد من مجلس الحكماء.

أخذ الوباء قرينته منذ سنوات, فلم يجد في القبيلة مخلوقا يصلح للمجالسة, ويؤتمن على السر, مثل عبده الذي ورثه عن أبيه.

يعود من المجلس الليلي منهكا. ينزع ثيابه الزرقاء. يستبدلها بالثياب البيضاء. يأخذ مكانه بجوار الركيزة. يسند ظهره الى العمود. يمد رجليه بموازاة المدخل. يتحرر من اللثام. يستدعي العبد. يأمره باشعال النار لإعداد رحيق «تيفوشكان» أو «تيبريمت» أو الخليط من العشبتين. وما أن ينطلق لسان النار من الموقد, وتتبدد الظلمة, حتى يتبدل الحال, وينطلق لسان النبيل أيضا, كما انطلق لسان النار.

في السنوات الأولى تحدث مع الجليس عن هموم الصحراء, وأحوال النساء, وأخبار العشاق, وأشعار الهجاء, ونوايا الأبكار. ولكن العقلاء ما لبثوا أن اختاروه عضوا في مجلسهم, خلفا لأبيه, فدأب على حضور المجمع الجليل, ورأى كيف تدبر المكائد بين الشيوخ , وعرف النوايا الخفية ضد القبائل المجاورة, ووقف على أساليب الزعيم في أبعاد الخلافات, وأنهاء الخصومات بين أعضاء المجلس, وأدرك أخيرا, أن أكثر العقلاء نفوذا وقدرا هم أكثرهم دهاء وقدرة على تدبير المؤامرات. فضاق صدره, وأصاب رأسه الدوار. في إحدى الليالي عاد الى الخباء واستدعى عبده العجوز. استبدل ثيابه. جرد سيفه من غمده. تألق النصل الشره في ضوء النار. خاطب العبد وهو يقلب في وجهه السلاح النهم: «الزعيم يجرد في وجوهنا سيفه ما أن ندخل خباء المجلس, ويتعمد أن يترك السيف خارج الغمد طوال الاجتماع. الزعيم يرى أن قوة القبيلة تقاس بقدرة عقلائها على كتمان سرها.

# Tongue

Each night when he came back from the meeting of tribal elders the nobleman would sit down and talk with his slave.

Years ago, disease had taken his wife from him and there was no one in the tribe as fit for sitting with—and confiding in—as the slave he'd inherited from his father. Returning completely exhausted from the evening council sessions, he would take off his blue robes, exchanging them for white ones. Taking his place next to the tent pole, he would lean back into it and stretch his feet parallel with the tent's entrance. Then, loosening the veil around his face, he would call out to the slave, ordering the man to stoke a fire and make a thick tea of wild green herbs. As soon as the tongues of the flame began to lick at the kindling, the night shadows began to dispel and the mood of the scene changed. And the nobleman's tongue would also begin to flicker and race like the fire itself.

During those first years, he spoke to his companion of the desert, of the ways of women, sharing as well poems of invective, reports of passionate lovers, and the schemes of eldest sons. The wise old men of the tribe had not hesitated when they chose him to replace his father as a member of their council. As he devoted himself to attending the illustrious convocation, he witnessed the sheikhs setting traps for one another and planning schemes against neighboring tribes. Though it seemed to him that the chief was adept at putting an end to disputes among members of the council, in the end, he realized that the most influential and powerful in the group were simply those who were the wiliest and most conniving.

This lesson was a blow to his heart and made his head spin.

One such evening, after returning to his tent and

calling his old slave, he pulled his sword from its sheath. Its ravenous blade flashed in the light of the flame. The nobleman began speaking, all the while turning the weapon over and over in the slave's face, "The chief waves his sword in *our* faces as soon as we enter the council meeting and leaves it conspicuously unsheathed throughout. He thinks that the strength of the tribe is measured by the ability of its leaders to keep secrets. If one of them talks, then the whole tribe risks annihilation. He leaves his sword hanging over our necks until the meeting is done. Listen carefully. Consider the edge of *this* blade—its tongue burns with a gnawing hunger keener than fire. If you repeat anything I have confided in you, its thirst will be quenched only by the blood of your neck. And yours is not the only blood that will be spilt—if any of the council's secrets ever get out, the chief's sword will also be drinking my blood!"

The old slave smiled an ambiguous smile—the kind understood only by clever herdsmen or slaves who have spent long years serving their masters. He leaned forward until the bottom fringe of his veil touched the half-charred acacia logs. The wood let out a plaintive sigh, and from it bubbled sticky, blood-colored sap.

The slave raised his head and murmured, "Never has it once occurred to me to dare to disobey an order from my master. But my master knows that his servant is no better than other creatures in the desert. The people of the desert have always suffered less from disease than they have from the poison of curiosity. I beseech you to forgive me for daring to ask you, Master, but spare me the misfortune of having to listen to the confidences of the illustrious council."

The nobleman watched the flame's tongue as it caressed the blade of the sword with threads of light and smiled. Soon, however, the smile darkened. Between them arose a deep silence, broken only by the moaning of the acacia wood. The nobleman finally said, "I am a widower. To whom then will I unburden myself? With no companion, with whom am I to sit and converse? Have you forgotten my father's instructions, which were the instructions of his father and grandfather before him? He warned me against mixing with the riff raff. You will remember that he did not warn me against loud braggarts simply because they are low creatures who know not loyalty. No. He warned me against them because their company is nothing but a trap that has already been set. Sitting and conversing with others is always a trap for the nobleman. When one sits with others, he has no choice but to surrender to the seduction. His tongue inevitably slips, and his mouth inevitably divulges something it ought not to, something detested by reason itself. I'm taking you as a sincere friend with whom I can converse so as to follow these instructions. I did not choose you as a vessel for storing my confidences because I've solved the mystery of the desert and discovered the hidden key of loyalty. No. I have chosen you because I have learned through experience that a slave who has faithfully served your father is better than the sincerest of friends. Bear with me as you bore with my father once upon a time. Incline your ears to me. And do not divulge any of my secrets lest it constrict my heart."

The slave breathed a sigh heavy with pain while his master leaned his back against the tent pole. From that day, the nobleman began to confide the secrets of the council as well as his own.

✣

Some months later, a scourge descended upon the nobleman's flock. At first, the malady struck the fierce camel he used to impregnate his she-camels. Huge and imposing, with a colossal hump that towered over his frame, the camel began to shrink and waste away until he was but skin and bones. In just a few months, the herders found the creature lying dead in the grazing pastures.

After that, a she-camel from a thoroughbred lineage was infected with the wasting disease and began to shrink and melt right in front of the herdsmen's eyes. They brought the matter to the nobleman's attention. He inspected her carefully, searching her body over for traces of the affliction, for symptoms of the malady, but could find no indications of what was wrong. When the she-camel also died, the nobleman decided to look for answers out in the pastures. He went around the various grazing fields, and interrogated the tribe's herders about the sickness. They all agreed: for years, the pastures had been free of disease. The men would then thrust their hands into the dirt, and chant sayings to repel the malice of the world. Turning their eyes toward the heavens, they would utter words of grace.

He then traveled to the neighboring tribe and returned with a blind doctor who was famous for his knowledge of animal maladies and for treating herd diseases. The doctor inspected the entire herd, animal by animal. He did not miss any of the he- or she-camels, not even the newborn. He found no symptoms of external diseases, nor any of internal infirmities. In the end, the doctor told the nobleman, "You need to search for the contagion in another place. It does not lie in the bodies of your livestock."

The nobleman asked, "Could it be a curse?"

"Perhaps."

At that moment, the nobleman was not aware that the mysterious contagion was laying a trap that would strike his prized thoroughbred camel, the piebald.

✤

This camel was very rare. The nobleman had received him as a gift from the chief of the Ifoghas tribes when he had been their guest. They were forming an alliance to stop one of the foreign invasions, and he had been carrying a message to their chief. He'd raised the animal himself, and cared for him as he'd never cared for his departed wife. The piebald had saved him from the trap set against him by the tribes of the southern jungles. When the water had run out in that labyrinth, that great sea of sand, the camel had carried him out alive. The dusty sands had blinded him, and he'd almost disappeared into the unknown. They'd shared a loyalty he'd never known among those false creatures who called themselves friends.

As the Mahri camel began to waste away, so did he. The camel rejected all food, and would not go out to the pastures. The nobleman also stopped eating, and refused to go out, even to the council meetings. He looked into the camel's kindly eyes and saw nothing there but sadness and worry. When his slave looked into his eyes, he saw the same things.

Weeks later, the Mahri thoroughbred died. The nobleman came down with a burning fever, and fell into a coma. The tribe thought he wouldn't come out of it.

It was during his initial recovery that he finally sent for the witch doctor.

The two men sat alone in the tent for an entire evening. The witch doctor left, and no one ever knew what had transpired between them. The following evening, out in the pastures, the herdsmen saw a shadow flitting about through the camels, but they assumed it was nothing more than a mischievous jinn, and paid it no attention.

Days later, the witch doctor paid him another visit. Again, the two conversed by themselves throughout the night. No one knew a thing about the strange man, of course. If people knew anything about him, he would not have been a witch doctor.

✣

Around the tribe, people said that it was the evil eye that had wiped out the nobleman's flock. It was envy, and none other, that had afflicted the piebald. The nobleman held his tongue. He slowly returned to attending the council of elders. He would sit next to the pole in his own tent and slide his sword from its sheath. And he made his faithful servant listen to the severe warning whenever he divulged the secrets of his heart and whenever he unburdened the weight of his soul. The loyal slave pleaded his case before his master time after time, urging the nobleman to spare him the burden of carrying his secrets. But suddenly, the old story took an unexpected turn.

Each night, after their conversation ended and after the last burning stick on the fire had gone out, the slave would leave the tent and disappear into the kingdom of shadow. His master never asked himself where the slave went. But that night, the nobleman waited for the slave to go off and, shortly after, prepared to follow him. The nobleman crept from the tent and walked into the dark. The slave went to the herd, and walked straight into their midst. He patted the head of one of the she-camels, then moved on. He kept walking, finally stopping in front of a fat camel covered with a thick coat of hair that was ravenously munching on dry grass. The camel stopped grazing and pricked up his ears. The creature's eyes grew tense and lost their composure. A sudden anxiousness arose in them.

The nobleman hid himself behind a nearby she-camel and began to watch. He studied the slave as the man sat down on the ground in front of the hairy camel. The slave then began to speak to the beast. The master listened as the slave repeated all the confidences that had been spoken about at the council. The very things that he had confided to the slave during that evening's session.

✤

The next morning, the nobleman examined the camel. He told the herders, "I don't need to be a fortune teller to tell you that this camel will be dead in a few weeks."

Only days later, the camel began to lose weight and waste away. Only a few weeks later, it died. The herders brought the news to him, their eyes filled with astonishment. He simply told them, "Now we know what's behind the disease."

He asked one of them to bring a whip from his tent. He asked the others to tie up his loyal servant and bring him as well. He took the whip in one hand and struck at the air with it. The weapon traced a loop through the air and snapped sparks like the lightning of a winter storm cloud. The sharp tongue of the whip landed on the slave, ripping apart his robe, tugging at the man's flesh. It licked and licked at the slave's body, while with each blow the nobleman yelled, "I won't let you go until you tell me how your sorcery killed my friend, the piebald." The slave cried out long and hard. He howled until his cries woke the entire desert.

At last, he asked his master to stop—he had decided to confess it all. He cried and cried for an hour, then sat drinking hot water for another. Finally, he spoke. "I did what I did out of my loyalty to you, Master! And out of my fealty to your father who never, from the moment he took me captive from the jungles, mistreated me."

The nobleman flicked the whip across the air, and

terror descended over them. He spoke, choking back his rage, "You dare to speak of loyalty—you who have most betrayed it? You speak of honoring the remains of the dead after despoiling those of the noblest creature in the entire tribe?"

The slave wept loudly, "I would not have done what I did, Master, if not for my faithfulness to you, and for the respect I have for the memory of your father. I told you, Master, that I did not deserve to be entrusted with your secrets because I am no divine being. Master, you know that even free men are incapable of guarding confidences, so how am I—a slave—supposed to be any better? If I did not unburden myself and divulge your secrets to mute creatures, I would have perished like your piebald died. Admit it, Master—you yourself could not bear your own secrets, and so decided to confide in your loyal servant. Wasn't it better for me to divulge your secrets, and those of the council, to creatures with ears but no tongues? Or should I have talked with the herdsmen who would have spread them from one to another around the tribe until they reached the ears of the chief? Despite the fact that my stupid deed killed my master's piebald, didn't it also protect him from the wrath of the chief?"

The slave started to howl again. The nobleman thought about the matter and then reached a decision. He pronounced the punishment, "Then I will cut out your tongue, you wretch."

The old slave pleaded, "Have mercy, my Lord! I'd rather you slit my throat than cut out my tongue."

The nobleman answered, "A man can slit his own throat, but he cannot remove his own tongue. Your tongue is the only thing that concerns me."

The old slave pleaded once more, "If I were able to slit my own throat, I wouldn't be a slave, Master. Kill me—but do not take my tongue."

The nobleman cut out the man's tongue.

And each night, when he came back from the council, he went back to sitting and talking to his slave, telling him all the secrets of the tribe.

After his master removed his tongue, the slave began to change into something else. He began to lose weight and waste away. But his master, who'd lost his companion the piebald, never stopped filling the man's ears with the most dangerous secrets. On top of these confidences the nobleman deliberately heaped sensitive information and news from the lands of neighboring tribes, as well as other intimacies of his own invention. The nobleman watched the sparkle that had seized the eyes of his slave, he noticed the trembling in the man's body and hands, and he heard the baffling sounds the slave uttered whenever he walked out of the tent following their evening session.

Some weeks later, the slave disappeared. The nobleman went to look for him in his tent and found him there leaning against the pole. Two empty eyes stared into the void. Swarms of flies covered his gaping mouth, as if trying to snatch from his lips a secret unspoken by the missing tongue. Even as he laid the body out on the ground and called for the herdsmen to prepare to shroud the body, the lips remained parted. And the empty tongueless mouth, a gaping wound.

# for daphne: lamented

Anja Utler | Translated by Kurt Beals from German (Germany)

Anja Utler was born in 1973 in Schwandorf, Germany, and now lives in Regensburg and Vienna. Her book *münden—entzüngeln*, published in 2004, won widespread critical acclaim. Thomas Poiss, in the Frankfurter Allgemeine Zeitung, called it "Utler's small but epochal masterpiece," and Paul Jandl, in the Neue Zürcher Zeitung, praised it as "an astonishingly smart and yet deeply sensuous book."

Utler's poetry stands out in part due to her unorthodox manipulation of language on both semantic and syntactic levels. In *münden—entzüngeln* this produces a blurring of the lines between body and nature, inside and outside. Thus *kiefer* may be both a pine tree and a jaw; "furcht" equivocates between the noun "fear" and the verb "furrows." The production of speech, too, is foregrounded, as the organs that produce sound blend with the world of which they speak: gorges, gullets and gullies, human tongues and tongues of land. The cumulative effect is a conflation of spheres, with multiple meanings operative at once. Utler's syntax adds to the ambiguity: punctuation breaks up lines in unexpected places, and parts of speech are often hard to pin down (particularly given the absence of German's usual tell-tale capitalization of nouns). Take the line "reiße noch bäume mich einmal…": "reiße noch bäume" could be understood as "[ich] reiße noch [die] bäume"— "i keep tearing [through] the trees." The "mich," though, introduces reflexivity, and Utler helpfully explained to me that the suggestion is "ich bäume mich auf"—"i rear up."

In this passage, Daphne, pursued by Apollo, is transformed into a laurel. Even as she struggles against the transformation, it has already taken hold. The presence of trees (*bäume*) in her rearing up (*bäume mich*) suggests that she cannot escape from this metamorphosis. The challenge for the translator, of course, is to bring about the metamorphosis of this complex text, with all its multiplicity of meanings, into an English poem with a similar range of connotations. Here I have tried to follow Utler's lead, transforming Daphne's limbs into the limbs of a tree, though the poem, like Daphne herself, does not bend easily to this metamorphosis.

Anja Utler's considerable formal innovations, together with her profoundly original exploration of the relationships between person, body, language, and nature, have already established her as an important voice in the German-speaking world and internationally. The selection here offers an impression of the striking—at times stark and unsettling—interplay of these elements in her work, as well as an attempt to find the English words that will weave them together with the subtlety and nuance of Utler's German.

Original text: Anja Utler, *münden—entzüngeln.* Vienna: Edition Korrespondenzen, Franz Hammerbacher, Copyright © 2004.

# für daphne: geklagt

*Im Lorbeer gewährt die verwandelte Daphne,*
*deren Name selbst den Lorbeer bezeichnet,*
*sich dem zum Dichter gewordenen Liebenden.*

KARLHEINZ STIERLE

*Der Seidelbast ist wie andere Daphnearten*
*sehr stark giftig. [..] Die Blätter ähneln im*
*Aussehen denen des Lorbeerbaumes, daher*
*der Gattungsname Daphne.*

EINTRAG UNTER:
www.heilpflanzen-suchmaschine.de

# for daphne: lamented

*Transformed into a laurel, Daphne,*
*whose own name denotes the laurel,*
*yields herself to the lover turned poet.*

KARLHEINZ STIERLE

*The spurge laurel, like other species of Daphne,*
*is highly poisonous. [..] The leaves resemble those of a*
*laurel tree, hence the genus name Daphne.*

ENTRY AT:
www.heilpflanzen-suchmaschine.de

mir selbst: wie entstachelt! von ihm als: habe sich alles
gedreht bin: gewittert, gepirscht jetzt – ganz: der gehetzte
schweiß – schnell ich: durch äste, gestrüpp ihm entstürzen
die: fangen zu greifen an haken gepeitscht mir – schneller –
die flanken augen – nein – (..) weiß: ich muss durch da muss
– schleunigst – hin an den fluss, fluss –

bitten ihn: nimm mich kurz, vater, ich: tunke mich dir
in die schnellen und du dann: entlasse mich – rein – als die gischt
ja, als luft, luft –
und ich kraus dir entfliehend als dank das gesicht –

ja, schon: spritzt du triffst: mir die fesseln – frischst –
wirst mich lösen, lassen – gleich, sofort –

myself: as if dethorned! by him as: if it had all
turned now am: scented, am stalked – fully: quarry my
sweat – rush: through branches, through brushwood from him
they: light into grab hook whipping – swifter –
my flanks eyes – no – (..) know: i must go through must
make it – at once – to the river, river –

✤

beg him: take me quick, father, i: plunge in your
rapids and you then: release me – pure – as foam
as air, air –
and fleeing i ripple your face in thanks –

✤

and, already: you spray: lap my ankles – refreshing –
will free me, let go – now, at once –

darf doch nicht – nein –
was: nimmst du dir –

selber – geradewegs – dir: auf den stickigen grund
gelaufen, festgesetzt: mit einem zug, ruck, nein,
reiße noch bäume mich einmal und stock –
muss: mich krümmen, ja kümmern: ins holz hinein
starren – was nimmst du mir: mich

✤

sehe, als letztes: das schmückt dich jetzt, ja, mein
erblindetes bild wird, muss immer, gekraust, mit dir glitzern
und trüber, ja linsig: so schwimmt es – dein dank –
auch dem treiber im blick

✤

wie trocken: mein arm macht – machte! die flanken, wie oft,
aufsprudeln, aus-
jetzt: nagen die, speicheln – bespringend – mich an –

may not though – no –
what: are you taking –

to you, ran – straight – onto your: sodden
ground, fixed: with a single jerk, lurch, no,
limbs ripping still rear up and stop –
i must: warp myself, withered, worked: into the wood
stiffen – what are you taking from me: me

✤

see, as last sight: it adorns you, my
unseeing image will, must always, glitter with you, rippled,
dimmer, now skimming: your thanks now – it swims –
in the eyes of the hunter as well

✤

how dry: my arm makes – made! the flanks, often, now they
well up, out

machen platz dann: rankt er sich mir zu: und sein heißes fleisch –

feucht! fortwährend – richtest dich auf in mir, mich:
dass ich stehe ja blühe und trage darf: nichtmal die blätter
lassen, mir fallen: nur früchte ab – unwillkürlich: so bring ich die –
rotten, nähren: dir deinen grund

weiter nur kümmern, dörren nur: dürsten zu dürfen
hören: ich raschle den vögeln jetzt trockener nach –

senge! bitte, dürre den schatten ihm: von dieser roten stirn,
dass er: ausglüht – ja mir: diesen puls aus den spitzen,
dass ich mich: auslöse – rein – als geruch als entknisternde
luft mich einsenke einsinke – laubend entlaubend mich –
in: die niedrigen, bastigen triebe und sie: enttreibe mir
kirschig, ja gischtig entstrecke – aufzischle: iss davon, iss –

they: salivate, gnaw – at me – mounting –
make room then: entwines himself in me: and his hot flesh –

damp! so unceasing – you rise up in me, raise me:
that i may stand, bloom and bear may: not even shed
leaves, just my: fruits fall away – unawares: so i bring them they –
rot, nourish: your ground

✤

now allowed just to wither, to parch just: to thirst
hear: i rustle out drier now after the birds –

singe! please, scorch the shadow from him: from this red brow,
so that he: may burn out – this pulse: from my tips,
so that i may: release myself – pure – as a scent as uncrackling
air may submerge may submerse – myself leafing deleafing –
into: the low, spurging shoots drive them: from me
berried, spraying, stretch out – hissing: eat of it, eat –

# From *At Shadow Flight*

Jacqueline Beaugé-Rosier | Translated by Gabrielle Civil from French (Haiti)

Born in 1932 in Jérémie, Jacqueline Beaugé-Rosier was educated in religious schools and spent her formative years training to be a nun. After clashing with the European sisters who ran the order, Beaugé-Rosier became an elementary school teacher. She also became a serious writer. A member of the Hougénikon literary group with Gérard Campfort, Phito Gracia, and others, she published her first collection of poems, *Les Climats en Marche,* in 1962.

Religious devotion, though, remained a key part of her vision. *A vol d'ombre* can be read as a love letter to God, in the form of *Abidhou*, the gull, the spiritual lover whose essence offers inner refuge from a country enshrouded in shadow. And at this moment in Haiti, all citizens—but especially intellectuals, artists, and journalists—live in the shadow of a crushing, palpable silence. Into silence, also, fellow writers, friends, and colleagues—including Phito Gracia—disappeared, never to be seen again.

Knowing this, *A vol d'ombre* appears especially urgent and extraordinary. Influenced by surrealism, the poem resonates with Négritude masterpieces by Aimé Césaire and René Depestre. With the political situation as a menacing backdrop, Beaugé-Rosier almost gushes with long-suffering desire. She veers from contemplative suffering to pleading passion, ending in mystical optimism.

Mixing abstraction and emotion in nearly every line, she both reveals and rewrites the silence.

Because Beaugé-Rosier's father supported Clément Jumelle, a main opponent of Duvalier in the 1957 election, her family was an early target. *A vol d'ombre*, originally published in Haiti in 1966 at the height of the first Duvalier dictatorship, names the shadow of Papa Doc's terror and transforms it into flight. After its publication Beaugé-Rosier had to go into hiding and ultimately emigrated to Canada in 1971.

Resettled, she has continued to write and has published *Cahiers de la mouette* (1983), *D'or vif et de pain* (1992), and *Les Yeaux de l'anse du Clair* (2001). *A vol d'ombre*, however, has remained long out of print.

For more than a dozen years, I have been both enchanted and daunted by the brilliance of this poem. Its French is dense, elegant, sincere, cerebral, and almost archaic at times in its formality. The poem is notoriously difficult to translate, yet the power of its language, its singularity and scale, have made the project indispensible.

When I asked Mme. Beaugé-Rosier, still living and writing in Ottawa, how she could write such an amazing poem in the midst of such repression, she answered, "It poured out of me, I had no choice." Humbled and inspired by the original, my translation arrives in the same spirit.

*The translator acknowledges the poet, her daughter Sandra Rosier, and poets Sun Yung Shin, Rachel Moritz, and Kristen Mason for their consultation on this translation.*

Original text: Jacqueline Beaugé-Rosier, *A vol d'ombre.*
Haiti: Collection *Hougénikon*, Imprimerie Serge L. Gaston, 1966.

# A vol d'ombre

Bientôt les pas frôleurs de la nuit
Auront contourné la veillée
Bientôt le lambi de vallées
Aura glapi de colère
Sans pitié je couperai le dialogue des pierres

Je n'irai plus auprès des bivouacs
Assoupir l'uniformité de ma honte
Par-delà les mains vrillées de perspectives
La danse progressive des ombres s'écroule

Rêve au déferlement des mers
Mon tourment de mouette
La geste rude la pensée figée
Passe le tour d'être à tes levres un supplice brutal
Mon absence lénitive à bien d'autres appels

# At Shadow Flight

Soon the gliding steps of the night
Will have circumvented the dusk
Soon the conch call of the valleys
Will have yelped in anger
Pitiless I will cut the dialogue of stones

I will go no more near the bivouacs
To lull the uniformity of my shame
Beyond hands twisted with perspectives
The progressive shadow dance collapses

Dream at the unfurling of seas
My torment of gull
The rough epic the arrested thought
Passes its turn to become at your lips a brutal torture
My absence soothing to many a call

Et mon verre avare de boire à ton verre
Ma citadelle déchue d'avoir à coups de pierre
Convergé sa défense
Tout ce qui m'attend le visage élargi d'humilité
Se joue de l'effet des scènes de la vie
Reprises à temps égal pour l'ondoiement multiple
Des fresques de ta vie

Tout ce qui m'attend
Chair broyée routes illuminées
Fleuves pacifiés
Les plaines dénudées de mon front géométrique
L'ont vu s'enflammer
D'équilibre

L'extase tue pour l'invite a changé
La forme compliquée de mon sourire

And my glass grudging to drink from your glass
My citadel collapsed after a hail of stones
Had it converge its defense
All that awaits me face broadened by humility
Easily making light of the scenes of life
Regularly reprised for the multiple baptism
Of the frescos of your life

All that awaits me
Ground flesh floodlit roads
Pacified rivers
The denuded plains of my geometric brow
Have seen it enflamed
In the balance

Ecstasy silenced as the invitation changed
The complicated shape of my smile

# A Thin Line Between Love and Hate

Adolfo Bioy Casares and Silvina Ocampo | Translated by Suzanne Jill Levine and Jessica Ernst Powell from Spanish (Argentina)

Adolfo Bioy Casares, born in Buenos Aires in 1914, was one of Argentina's most celebrated writers. His books include *The Invention of Morel*, about which Jorge Luis Borges said, "to classify it as perfect is neither an imprecision nor a hyperbole." Among his other novels, *Asleep in the Sun, Plan for Escape,* and *The Adventures of a Photographer in La Plata* have been translated by Suzanne Jill Levine, who also edited his *Selected Stories* and translated *A Russian Doll and Other Stories*. A lifelong friend of Borges, Bioy was also Borges' most constant collaborator and the two of them even created a third writer, called Biorges, by the critic Emir Rodriguez Monegal, who wrote parodic detective stories under pseudonyms including H. Bustos Domecq and Suarez Lynch (these names were real family names from the ancestors of both writers).

Silvina Ocampo, born in 1903, was also a highly respected figure in the Argentine literary world, and was a prolific poet as well as a writer of short stories marked by an oblique eroticism and perversely surreal humor. Bioy Casares and Ocampo met through Bioy Casares's mother Marta and Ocampo's elder sister, Victoria Ocampo, who edited the influential Argentine literary magazine *Sur*, and Silvina and Adolfo were married in 1940.

*Los que aman, odian* (A Thin Line Between Love and Hate) is the only novella Adolfo Bioy Casares and Silvina Ocampo collaborated on. Written in 1946, this tongue-in-cheek detective romp at a seaside resort involves typically Eurocentric Argentines, love intrigues, a dead body, a disappearance, allusions to WWII, and a whole gamut of literary winks. This collaboration with Ocampo was similar in spirit to the detective parodies that Bioy Casares and Borges were forging in the 1940s, and is also a kind of roman à clef about the real couple's romantic foibles.

Because of his wry depictions, Bioy Casares's narrators and characters tend to invite a reader's laughter unexpectedly: no matter how hard they seek to be dignified, their actions and utterances appear mildly buffoonish. The protagonist of this collaboration with Ocampo is a worthy buffoon of similar ilk—Dr. Humberto Huberman is pretentious, fastidious, self-important and apparently completely unaware of his own fussy affectations. For the reader, this makes him a slightly ridiculous and often unwittingly hilarious figure. Dr. Huberman is, in many respects, representative of a particular type of Argentine intellectual (a self-parody of the authors, perhaps?) and for the translator (in this case two collaborators who giggled as they strove for the words and phrasing that would create the intended effect) this means the challenge of seeking those nuances that will make him recognizably funny to a non-Argentine reader.

Original text: Adolfo Bioy Casares and Silvina Ocampo, *Los que aman, odian*. Buenos Aires: Emecé, 1946.

# Los que aman, odian

1

Se disuelven en mi boca, insípidamente, reconfortantemente, los últimos glóbulos de arsénico (*arsenicum album*). A mi izquierda, en la mesa de trabajo, tengo un ejemplar, en hermoso Bodoni, del *Satyricón*, de Cayo Petronio. A mi derecha, la fragante bandeja del té, con sus delicadas porcelanas y sus frascos nutritivos. Diríase que las páginas del libro están gastadas por lecturas innumerables; el té es de China; las tostadas son quebradizas y tenues; la miel es de abejas que han libado flores de acacias, de favoritas y de lilas. Así, en este limitado paraíso, empezaré a escribir la historia del asesinato de Bosque del Mar.

Desde mi punto de vista, el primer capítulo transcurre en un salón comedor, en el tren nocturno a Salinas. Compartían mi mesa un matrimonio amigo—diletantes en literatura y afortunados en ganadería y una innominada señorita. Estimulado por el *consommé*, les detallé mis propósitos: en busca de una delcitable y fecunda soledad —es decir, en busca de mí mismo—yo me dirigía a ese nuevo balneario que habíamos descubierto los más refinados entusiastas de la vida junto a la naturaleza: Bosque del Mar. Desde hacía tiempo acariciaba yo ese proyecto, pero las exigencias del consultorio—pertenezco, debo confesarlo, a la cofradía de Hipocrates—postergaban mis vacaciones. El matrimonio asimiló con interés mi franca declaratión: aunque yo era un médico respetable—sigo invariablemente los pasos de Hahnemann — escribía con variada fortuna argumentos para el cinematógrafo. Ahora la Gaucho Film, Inc. me encarga la adaptatión, a la época actual y a la escena argentina, del tumultuoso libro de Petronio. Una reclusión en la playa era imprescindible.

Nos retiramos a nuestros compartimientos...

# A Thin Line Between Love and Hate

## 1

The last drops of arsenic (*arsenicum album*) dissolve in my mouth, insipidly, comfortingly. To my left, on the desk, is the copy—a beautiful Bodoni—of Gaius Petronius's *Satyricon*; to my right, the fragrant tea tray with its delicate chinaware and its nutritive jars. Suffice it to say that the book's pages are well worn from innumerable readings; the tea is from China; the toast is crisp and delicate; the honey is from bees that have sipped the nectar of acacia flowers and lilacs. And so, in this encapsulated paradise, I shall begin to write the story of the murder at Bosque del Mar.

To my way of thinking, the first chapter begins in a dining car on the night train to Salinas. Sharing my table sat a couple who were friends of mine—who dabbled in literature and were fortunate with livestock—and a nameless young woman. Bolstered by the *consommé*, I explained my intentions: in search of a delectable and fruitful solitude—that is to say, in search of myself—I was on my way to the new seaside resort discovered by the most refined nature enthusiasts amongst us: Bosque del Mar. I had cherished the idea of this trip for some time now, but the demands of the office—I belong, I must admit, to the brotherhood of Hippocrates—had postponed my vacation. The married couple reacted with interest to my frank declaration: although I was a respected physician—and a loyal disciple of Hahnemann—I also wrote screenplays, with varying degrees of success. Now Gaucho Films, Inc. had commissioned me to write an adaptation of Petronius's tumultuous book, set in present-day Argentina. Seclusion at the beach was *de rigueur.*

We returned to our compartments. A short time later,

I was enveloped in thick railway blankets as my spirit still sang with the pleasurable sensation of having been understood. A sudden doubt tempered my joy: had I acted rashly? Had I just handed, to that amateur couple, all the materials required to steal my ideas? I knew that it was useless to dwell upon this. My spirit, ever malleable, sought refuge in the anticipated contemplation of the trees by the ocean. A pointless effort: I was still a night away from those pine groves... Like Betteredge with *Robinson Crusoe*, I resorted to my Petronius. I read this paragraph with renewed admiration:

> This is why I believe that our hapless youngsters are turned into total idiots in the schools of rhetoric, because their ears and eyes are trained not on everyday issues, but on pirates in chains on the sea-shore, or on tyrants signing edicts bidding sons decapitate their fathers, or on oracular responses in time of plague urging the sacrifice of three or more maidens...

The advice is still valid today. When will we at last renounce the detective novel, the fantasy novel, and the entire prolific, varied, and ambitious literary genre that is fed by unreality? When will we return to the path of the salubrious picaresque and pleasant local color?

The sea air had begun to filter through the window. I closed it. I fell asleep.

## 2

Following my instructions to the letter, the steward woke me at six in the morning. I performed a few brief ablutions with the remainder of the bottle of Villavicencio water that I had requested before retiring the night before, took ten drops of arsenic, dressed, and went to the dining car. My breakfast consisted of a fruit salad and two cups of *café con leche* (we must remember, alas, that the tea on trains is from Ceylon). I was sorry not to have the opportunity to explain a few details of intellectual property law to the couple with whom I had dined the previous evening; they were going much further than Salinas (known these days as Colonel Faustino Tambussi), and, undoubtedly intoxicated by the effects of an allopathic pharmacopoeia, they were giving over to sleep these liminal morning hours which are, thanks to our native indolence, the exclusive province of country folk.

Running nineteen minutes behind schedule—at 7:02—the train arrived in Salinas. No one assisted me with my luggage. The stationmaster—as far as I could tell, the only person awake in the entire town—was too engrossed in a childish game of tossing wicker hoops with the engineer to help a solitary traveler, oppressed by time and luggage. At length he finished his dealings with the engineer and walked over to me. I am not a resentful person, and had already arranged my mouth in a friendly smile and was reaching for my hat when, like a lunatic, he set upon the freight car door. He opened it, lunged inside, and I saw five clamorous bird cages tumble into a heap on the platform. I was choked with indignation. I would have gladly offered to take charge of the hens in order to save them from such violence. I consoled myself with the thought that more merciful hands had wrestled with my suitcases.

I turned quickly toward the station yard in order to confirm that the hotel car had arrived. It had not. Immediately, I decided to question the stationmaster. After looking for a while, I found him sitting in the waiting room.

"Are you looking for something?" he asked me.

I did not disguise my impatience.

"I am looking for you."

"Well then, here I am."

"I am waiting for the car from the Hotel Central, in Bosque del Mar."

"If you don't mind a bit of company, I suggest that you take a seat. At least here there's a bit of a breeze." He consulted his watch. "It's 7:14 and already this hot. I'll be honest with you: this will end in a storm."

He took a small mother-of-pearl penknife from his pocket and began to clean his fingernails. I asked him if the hotel car would be much longer. He replied:

"My forecasts do not cover that issue."

He continued his work with the penknife.

"Where is the post office?" I asked.

"Go to the water pump, beyond the railcars on the dead-end track. Past the tree on your right-hand side, turn at a right angle, cross in front of Zubeida's house and don't stop until you get to the bakery. The tin hut is the post office." My informant traced the details of the trajectory in the air with his hands. Then he added: "If you find the boss awake, I'll give you a prize."

I indicated where I'd left my luggage, begged him not to allow the hotel car to leave without me, and set forth into that sprawling labyrinth, under a blazing sun.

## 3

Feeling much relieved by the precise instructions I had given—all correspondence in my name should be forwarded to the hotel—I embarked on my return. I stopped at the water pump and, after some rather vigorous exertion, managed to stave off my thirst and to wet my head with two or three splashes of tepid water. Proceeding unsteadily, I arrived at the station.

In front sat an old Rickenbacker, loaded with the chicken cages. How much longer would I be forced to wait in this inferno for the hotel car to come collect me?

In the waiting room I found the stationmaster speaking with a man in a thick leather jacket. The man asked me:

"Doctor Humberto Huberman?" I nodded. The stationmaster said:

"We'll load your luggage now."

It is incredible how much happiness these words afforded me. Without too much trouble I managed to settle in among the chicken cages. We began our journey toward Bosque del Mar.

The first fifteen miles of the road consisted of a series of potholes; the admirable Rickenbacker progressed slowly and hazardously. I looked for the sea, like a Greek advancing on Troy: not a single trace of purity in the air seemed to announce its proximity. Clustered around a water trough, a flock of sheep tried to find shelter from the sun in the feeble rays of shade cast by a windmill. My traveling companions stirred in their cages. Each time the car came to a stop at a gate, a dusting of feathers would spread through the air like flower pollen, and an ephemeral olfactory sensation would remind me of a happy episode of my childhood, with my parents in my uncle's henhouses in Burzaco. Might I confess that for a few moments I took refuge, in the midst of the jostling and the heat, in the pristine vision of a boiled egg set in a white porcelain teacup?

At last we came to a range of sand dunes. In the distance I made out a crystalline fringe. I greeted the sea: *Thalassa!... Thalassa!...* It was a mirage. Forty minutes later I saw a wine dark expanse. Inwardly, I yelled: *Epi oinopa ponton!* I turned to the *chauffeur*.

"This time I am not mistaken. There is the sea."

"It's a field of purple flowers," he replied.

A short while later I noticed that the potholes had ceased. The *chauffeur* told me:

"We must go quickly. The tide comes up in a few hours."

I looked around. We were advancing slowly over some thick planks, in the middle of a stretch of sand. The sea appeared in the distance, between the sand dunes to the right. I asked:

"Well, then, why are you going so slowly?"

"If a tire goes off the planks, we will be buried in the sand."

I did not want to think about what would happen were we to encounter another automobile. I was too tired to worry. I didn't even notice the cool sea air. I managed to formulate the question:

"Are we nearly there?"

"No," he replied. "It's twenty-five miles from here."

---

Page 174, The English version of the quoted passage is taken from P. G. Walsh's translation of *The Satyricon* (Oxford University Press, 1999), Chapter 1 "At the School of Rhetoric," Paragraph 1.

# W. The Death of Idealism

Tan Chee Lay | Translated by Teng Qian Xi from Chinese (Singapore)

It was the superbly surrealistic exploration of political themes in this sequence, from his collection *Zao Jian Di* (Where Swords Are Forged), that prompted my interest in Singaporean poet Tan Chee Lay's work. "W. The Death of Idealism" is part of the sequence "Myths of T Century," where the letters marking each title complete the word "Taiwan." The dates named in this poem refer to the Tiananmen massacre in China, when tanks and soldiers rolled into Tiananmen Square in the late hours of June 3rd through 4th 1989, as a final attempt to crush protesters calling for democratic reform.

The consequences of such idealism are at the heart of Tan's poem. He compares ideals to "a sailor's rope" and "a hunter's bow"—tools that human beings devise to attempt to control the natural world, but which are ultimately powerless. There is no space for ideals; even desire does not create a sanctuary from the controls imposed by society. The addressee is framed as being as relentless as the forces of nature, with a gaze that is "a raft a thousand miles away" from the ideals floundering "in death's sea."

This poem sanctifies none of the parties in the tragedy; it is clear that those who have been "raped by civilization" are, like the student protesters, a part of it. Their origins as individuals living under oppressive systems were already rooted in violence, and they cannot avoid this knowledge. These images become particularly poignant when we remember that the civilian protesters at Tiananmen were, in most accounts, led by students from the elite Beijing University who often used the rhetoric of childhood innocence in their speeches to rally people to their cause.

Yet we are reminded that the leaders of the protests were, after all, being groomed to be part of the political elite:

> I worry that the baby unable to find a breast
> will, amidst her howls, see through
> the maternal instinct

In his original, Tan uses the phrase "宝宝" (bǎo bǎo), a collective noun which could denote babies in the plural or singular, and does not specify gender. I have chosen to translate it as referring to a female infant, since the impact of the image is, I feel, deepened when the baby is not just a recipient of "the maternal instinct," but will also be pressured to conform to essentialist ideas that she recognizes as a myth.

The speaker's "worry" is understandable, given the perils faced by idealists, on which the poem has dwelled so graphically. On the other hand, perhaps these are an unavoidable part of "diverting [one's] vessel towards life," and doing one's part to counter the violence that various components of "civilization" are still inflicting on the lives of people all over the world.

Original text: Tan Chee Lay, *Zao Jian Di*. Singapore: firstfruits publications, 2002.

# W. 理想主意阵亡

请不要以为在六月四日
寄上一封限时挂号
就 PS 附上了慎重和愧疚

我的信箱早已封锁，荒芜
里头只静卧着一封
与邮差绝交书
奄奄一息

当然
你曾经是海上飘来的水雾
我是意大利水手的双耳
有不能自拔的聆听，在风中颤抖
而当我将生活转舵
海盗船　暴风雨　龙卷风　暗流　险滩
航线早已注定
波浪必定崎岖

你必须承认
曾遭文明强暴已不是处女之身——
曾在凌晨怀孕　傍晚堕胎　子夜上吊
命运不会领养一个不知生父的私生子

我担心找不到乳房的宝宝
在啼哭中，会看清
母性

我清醒于六月三日的深夜
理想之必然
如水手的绳索，猎人的弓
浪很凶，兽性很普及
水手投海，猎人自刎

# W. The Death of Idealism

please don't think that sending a registered letter
on the fourth of June
entails a postscript of gravity and guilt

my mailbox has long been locked, barren
in it rests one letter only
severing bonds with the postman
in its last breath

of course
once you were the mist drifting at sea
I was an Italian sailor's ears
compulsively listening, quivering in the wind
and when I diverted my vessel towards life
there were pirate ships    storms
    cyclones    whirlpools    perilous shores
routes already determined
waves compelled to heave

you must acknowledge
that those raped by civilization were no longer virgins—
they conceived at dawn    miscarried at dusk
    hanged themselves at midnight
fate will not raise a bastard
who does not know his real father

I worry that the baby unable to find a breast
will, amidst her howls, see through
the maternal instinct

I woke in the wee hours of the third of June
ideals are as inescapable

下场之必然，如你
理想在死亡之海中沉浮
你的回眸是一块万里外的浮板
且越　　飘　　　越　　　　模　　　　　　　糊

六月五日凌晨
我是背负着十字架的船身
让所有属风的向风认错
让所有属浪的随浪灭顶
让所有航行的
都对水的倒影负责

后现代的海峡
没有所谓的自由水域
在情欲的风浪中和理想恋爱
你我之间
唯有
禁欲主义

as a sailor's rope a hunter's bow
the waves are fierce brutality has spread
the sailor is engulfed the hunter cuts his own throat
these endings inevitable, like you
ideals are bobbing in death's sea
your backward glance a raft a thousand miles away
floating growing more and more obscure

dawn the fifth of June
I was a boat carrying a crucifix
let those of the air confess to the winds
let those of the sea collapse with the waves
let those travelling by ship answer to
reflections in the sea

in the straits of postmodernity
there are no so-called stateless waters
while wooing ideals in desire's tempests
between you and me
abstinence
is all there is

# In promptu

Martín Adán | Translated by Rick London and Katherine Silver from Spanish (Peru)

Martín Adán was born Rafael de la Fuente Benavides in Lima, Peru, in 1908. After attending the Deutsche Schule in Lima, Adán studied at the National University of San Marcos in Lima, completing his doctoral thesis *De lo barroco en el Peru* (Concerning the Baroque in Peru) in 1938. While employed by the legal department of the Agricultural Bank, he worked on a critical/biographical dictionary of Peruvian letters, which went unfinished.

Adán suffered a breakdown in the early 1940s. He was admitted to a private clinic where he was intermittently confined throughout his adult life, and where he died in 1985. He became a member of the Peruvian Academy of Language during confinement there.

Adán was awarded the José Santos Chocano National Prize for poetry in 1946 and the National Prize for Literature in 1976.

Although personally isolated for much of his life, Adán's world included a vast resource of world literature, and his isolation and erudition combined to form a startling hermeticism. This visionary poetry is unique and, at times, eccentric, seemingly not part of any local conversation. Adán's writing is more reminiscent of Mallarmé or Wallace Stevens than any of the main proponents of *modernismo*.

"In promptu," the Latin title of a Chopin piano work, comes from Adán's poetry collection *Travesía de*

*Extramares* (Crossing to Other Seas), published in 1950, and is part of a sequence of sonnets using the figure of Chopin to invoke a cosmic muse. It is a poetry that confronts presumed meaning and the way the mind makes meaning, often by means of a density and volatility of images that keep the poetic field from resolving in any terms. Adán will use a word as a talisman, evocative and incantatory, primarily free of conventional lexical or visual information.

These poems invite in energies from "beyond the limits of the normal world" (Eliot) and allow the mind a glimpse of its own vast possibilities. Adán explored his art freely, with little regard for the reader. Indeed, his shifts and juxtapositions, his grammatical dislocations and invented words, create tensions that can cause the intelligibility of the text to tremble, even as he weaves it into lovely song. The translation that follows attempts to balance the lyric coherence of the poem with the semantic and syntactic synesthesia it effects.

RICK LONDON

Original text: Martín Adán, *Travesía de Extramares (Sonetos a Chopin)*. Lima, 1950.

# In promptu

*Aquí no hay*
*sino ver y desear;*
*aquí no veo*
*sino morir con deseo.*
CASTILLEJO

*Poor soul, the center of*
*my sinful earth.*
SHAKESPEARE

—Cual al aire la araña, hila que hila,
Teje que teje sombra y apretura,
Impromptu trama äcre en cuadratura
De la voz más sabrosa y más tranquila:

«—La luna que en la onda se deshila…
El accorde, siniestro, que perdura…
La quijada, que aún de amor murmura…
El seto vivo que en panteón copila…»

—¡Fuera lo otro, de réplica y trociente!...
¡Música úrdase sola y simplemente,
Sin nombre, sin memoria, sin mañana!...

—¡Evad, que, si cantare la figura,
Disonará, divina, ïnhumana:
«Toda imagen es de tu desventura»!

# In promptu

*Here there is*
*only seeing and desiring;*
*here I see*
*only dying of desire.*
CASTILLEJO

*Poor soul, the center of*
*my sinful earth.*
SHAKESPEARE

Unto the air the spider, spinning and spinning,
Weaving and weaving shadow and constriction,
Impromptu weft, bitter in its quadrature,
Most peaceful and delicious voice:

"The moon unraveled by the wave . . .
The sinister chord that lasts . . .
The jaw that still whispers of love . . .
The hedge that gathers in a graveyard . . ."

Away with the other, dismembered and fake . . .
Music threads itself alone and simply,
Without name, without memory, without tomorrow . . .

Beware, for if the figure sings
It will be unharmonious, divine, inhuman:
"All images are of your misfortune."

# Writing

Aleksandr Skidan | Translated by Rebecca Bella from Russian (Russia)

Aleksandr Skidan was born in Leningrad in 1965. He is a poet, translator, cultural critic, and member of the working group "Chto Delat?" ("What Is to Be Done?"). His books include *Delirium*, *In the Re-Reading* and *Red Shifting*, for which he received the prestigious Andrei Bely Prize in 2006, and which was published in English by Ugly Duckling Presse in 2008. His poetry has been translated into multiple languages, and he himself is a translator of poetry (Charles Olsen, Eileen Myles) and theory.

In the prose poems, Skidan follows the traces of human artifacts like tracks in the snow. When I first began to translate these poems, I felt that these traces were indeed obscured by the solid block of the prose itself. Without a shape on the page that said *poem*, I worried that I would have trouble creating the feeling of a poem in English. Yet, as we worked, I discovered that these prose poems, many of which are inspired by artists in Skidan's community, map the nonlinear process of art-making rather than charting a simple path from one line to the next.

Each poem begins with what is usually seen as an end-point—a work of art in a gallery, a specimen in a museum, a poem, or a translation, and Skidan follows the trail of the artwork both backward—to the creative cycle of the artist, the provenance of the materials, and ultimately to the original beginnings, immaculate conception or the big bang—and forward, towards diminishment, death throes, and oblivion. Thus, the material artifact encompasses the very edges of being, and the border with non-reason and infinite non-being. In this exploration, the art of writing occupies a special position, because, unlike material art forms, it carries conceptual thought and the ability, or responsibility, to approach "intimately close to one's own death." Thus the poet is sensitive to the greatest concern: the end of life, consciousness, and time. In the midst of this material life, Skidan follows the tracks and leads us to contemplate the outer realms of physics and philosophy. The experience is both strenuous and disarming.

Original text: Aleksandr Skidan, "Pis'mo."
[Previously unpublished.]

# ПИСЬМО

И «я» в моем теплом теле знает: он разом хочет и умереть и быть. И это хотение так захлестывает, так приводит его, что он проваливается по всем статьям, как если бы провал действительно был, был тем, чего он безусловно желал, как желают, как лелеют жало пустого сна; наконец, как если бы такое проваливание, под стать медленному удовольствию падать отпущенным, означало круговую поруку, в которой некто еще может за него поручиться: его не убудет. Не когда, а куда умрешь, говорят ему. То есть, не умереть к бытию, что было бы ослеплением, простой инверсией просветления бытия к смерти, но схватиться с велеречивым спазмом за тень листа, за поверхность присутствия. Он утруждает себя в ручном труде, заблуждением. Ведь как раз таки письмо и настаивает на отсутствии в настоящем уст, ответственных произнести «я» нераздельно, слитно, оно, это «я», схлопывается в корешок книги, как во тьму рукава, готового выпростать из своих фиктивных глубин трещетку китайского веера, где один и тот же подернутый странной дымкой пейзаж разбит на неуловимо различающиеся фрагменты. Расщепление письмом стирает ненасытную субъективность, и не в силу наносимого ей увечья или распыления монологической установки, а по причине вхождения в интимную близость с собственной смертью. Каковая не отдается здесь ни малейшим эхом. Она есть причинение ничто, неприемлемый дар такого

# Writing

And the "I" in my warm flesh knows: he wants both to die and to be. And this wanting so whips him, so grips him, that he fails in all arenas, as if this failure were real, as if that were what he undoubtedly desired, as one desires, as one cherishes the sting of an unreadable dream; at last, as if such failure, the slow pleasure of freefall, meant mutual protection, where someone could still guarantee: nothing will happen to you. It's not *when* you die, but *where* you die *to*, they tell him. That is, not to die toward being, as this would be a blinding, a simple inversion of the enlightenment of being towards death, but to seize, with a high-sounding spasm, the shadow of the page, the surface of existence. He troubles himself with handwork, daydreaming. For it's writing itself that insists on the absence from reality of the mouths that pronounce "I" undivided, slurred, conjoined, this "I" folds into the spine of a book, as if into the murk of a sleeve that is poised to release, from its fictive depths, the rattle of a Chinese fan, whose strange, stretched, hazy landscape is divided into irretrievable separate fragments. The fission in the text erases this insatiable subjectivity, not with injurious force or by dispersion of the monologic conceit, but by approaching intimately close to one's own death. Which doesn't yield the smallest echo. It's the infliction of nothingness, the unacceptable gift of forgetfulness, which allows you, without coming closer, to reach a point where it's no longer possible to be able, no longer possible to surmount and to grasp, and therefore, to think. Forgive him. Then, and

беспамятства, которое позволяет, не приближаясь, приблизиться к точке, где больше уже невозможно мочь, невозможно превозмочь и схватить и, следовательно, помыслить. … Простите ему. Тогда, и только тогда, когда отнимается и эта последняя власть, когда вся тайна мира оказывается заключенной в простое вот, не способное даже взывать к окоченевшим зрачкам, в коих шелушится, продолжая мерещиться, слово Бог, тогда начинает простираться стирание. Бесследное и окончательное, поверх «я», поверх книги; в его присном присутствии. Медленный яд. Письмо, стало быть, и есть то, что неустанно пробуждает к забвению.

only then, when this last power is gone, when all the mystery of the world is reduced to one simple *there*, that can't even summon the numbing pupil, in which the word "God," still ghostly apparent, rustles, *then* begins the long erasure. Traceless and final, beyond "I," outside the book; in its eternal presence. Slow poison. It is writing, then, which tirelessly awakens to oblivion.

# Smell

Saadat Hasan Manto | Translated by Aftab Ahmad and Matt Reeck from Urdu (India)

Saadat Hasan Manto (1912-55) is perhaps the best-known Modernist fiction writer in South Asia. His stories won him censure during his lifetime, and since his death his partition stories have been widely cited by South Asian writers and used in classrooms to help students come to some understanding of the atrocities of 1947. His stories that take place in Bombay, including "Smell," offer another view of the times—full of the characters of pulp fiction, they depict a seedy world of opportunity, ambiguous morals, and cosmopolitan energy.

Manto is considered a peripheral member of the Progressive Writers Movement—the most important literary movement of his times—whose members advocated a "literature that trains its eye upon the realities of life, reflects them, investigates them and leads the way toward a new and better life." (Azami 1972, 46) While Manto never referred to himself as a Progressive writer, nonetheless he shared an interest in the lower strata of South Asian society and was friends with many writers of the movement, most notably Krishan Chander and Ismat Chughtai. That being said, the group's official reaction to "Smell" shows the hostility with which the movement's doctrinaire members treated him. In the All India Urdu Congress in Hyderabad in 1944, Sajjad Zahir, one of the founding members, criticized the story not only for being obscene but also for not having the reformatory intent that modern fiction should have. Literature was meant to be a vehicle for social uplift, and "Smell," like the majority of Manto's stories, fell short of that.

In fact this story and his essay "Modern Literature" were the texts that led to his third obscenity trial (there were five in all). In the manner typical of these trials, he was convicted in the lower court but then acquitted in sessions court. On May 3, 1945, Special Sessions' Judge Mr. M.R. Bhatiya wrote in his judgment "there was nothing to incite lustful feelings, and moreover in the testimony of the expert literary witnesses the story is progressive ... and will have no harmful effect on people's morals."

Manto's strengths include his willingness to push against the norms of the literary establishment, such as with the sensuous focus and class reversals of "Smell"; in other stories, his characters, dialogue and fast-moving situational writing reflect a cineaste's keen sense of scene and intrigue (he also wrote scripts for the film industry). On the other hand, his metaphoric descriptions often test the American reader. For example, when Randhir snaps off the *ghatin* (a particularly low Christian caste) woman's bra, Manto likens her breasts to "a potter's newly turned vessels." Then he extends this simile in a somewhat disconcerting direction: "just beneath the skin there seemed to be a layer of faint light giving off a spectral glow like how a pond can radiate light from beneath its turgid surface." Perhaps the analogy goes too far, and yet the thrill of the story lies in the ambivalence of the faintly repellent but more powerfully alluring body of this low-class woman.

---

Page 194, quote from: Azami, Khalil ur-Rahman. *Urdu men taraqqi pasand adabi tahrik*. Aligarh: Anjuman Taraqqi. 1972. 46, 67.

Original text: Saadat Hasan Manto, "bu" from *Lazzat-e-sang*. Lahore: Naya Idarah, 1948.

# بو

برسات کے یہی دن تھے۔ کھڑکی کے باہر پیپل کے پتے اِسی طرح نہا رہے تھے۔ ساگوان کے اس اسپرنگو ں والے پلنگ پر جو اب کھڑکی کے پاس سے ذرا ادھر کو سرکا دیا گیا تھا۔ ایک گھا ٹن لونڈیا رندھیر کے ساتھ چمٹی ہو ئی تھی۔

کھڑکی کے باہر پیپل کے پتے رات کے دودھیالے اندھیرے میں جھمکو ں کی طرح تھر تھرا رہے تھے، اورنہا رہے تھے، اور وہ گھا ٹن لو نڈیا رندھیر کے ساتھ کپکپاہٹ بن کر چمٹی تھی۔ شام کے قریب دن بھر ایک انگریزی اخبار کی تمام خبریں اور اشتہار پڑھنے کے بعد جب وہ بالکنی میں ذرا تفریح کی خاطر آکھڑا ہوا تھا تو اس نے اس گھا ٹن لڑکی کو جو غالباً ساتھ والے رسیو ں کے کارخانے میں کام کرتی تھی اور بارش سے بچنے کے لیے اِملی کے درخت کے نیچے کھڑی تھی، کھانس کھنکھار اپنی طرف متو جہ کیا تھا۔ اور آخر میں ہاتھ کے اشارے سے اسے اوپر بلا لیا تھا۔

وہ کئی دنوں سے شدید قسم کی تنہا ئی محسوس کر رہا تھا۔ جنگ کے با عث بمبئی کی تقریباً تمام کرسچیئن چھو کریا ں، جو پہلے سستے داموں پر مل جاتی تھیں، عورتو ں کی اگزالری فورس میں بھرتی ہو گئی تھیں۔ ان میں سے بعض نے فورٹ کے علا قے میں ڈانسنگ اسکول کھول لیے تھے، جہا ں صرف فوجی گورو ں کو جانے کی اجازت تھی—رندھیر بہت اُداس ہو گیا تھا۔ اس کی اُداسی کی ایک وجہ تو یہ تھی کہ کرسچیئن چھو کریا ں نایاب ہو گئ تھیں۔ دوسری وجہ یہ بھی تھی کہ رندھیر، جو فوجی گورو ں کے مقابلے میں کہیں زیادہ مہذب، تعلیم یا فتہ، صحت مند اور خوبصورت تھا، صرف اس لیے اس پر فورٹ کے اکثر قحبہ خانو ں کے دروازے بند کر د ئیے گئے تھے کہ اُس کی چمڑی سفید نہیں تھی۔

جنگ سے پہلے رندھیر ناگپا ڑہ اور تا ج ہو ٹل کے گردو نو ا ح کی کئ کرسچئین لڑکیو ں سے جسمانی ملا قات کر چکا تھا۔ اُسے اچھی طرح معلو م تھا کہ ایسی ملا قات کے آداب سے وہ ان کرسچئین لو نڈوں کے مقابلے کہیں زیا دہ واقفیت رکھتا ہے جن سے یہ لڑکیا ں فیشن کے طور پر رومانس لڑا تی ہیں اور بعد میں کسی چغد سے شادی کرلیتی ہیں ۔

رندھیر نے محض دل ہی دل میں ہیزل سے اس کی تازہ تازہ پیدہ شدہ رعونت کا بدلہ اس گھا ٹن لڑکی کو اشارے سے اوپر بلا یا تھا۔ ہیزل اس کے فلیٹ لینے کی خاطر کے نیچے رہتی تھی اور ہر روز صبح کو وردی پہن کر اور اپنے کٹے ہو ئے بالوں پر خاکی رنگ کی ٹو پی ترچھے زاویے پر جما کر باہر نکلتی تھی، اور اس اندازسے چلتی تھی گو یا فٹ پاتھ پر تمام جانے والے اس کے قدمو ں کے آگے ٹاٹ کی طرح بچھتے چلے جا ئیں گے۔

# Smell

1

It was a monsoon day just like today. Outside the window the leaves of the pipal tree were glistening in the rain, just as they are now. On this very teak bed, now pushed back a little from where it used to rest next to the window, a *ghatin* girl was nuzzling against Randhir's side.

Outside the window the leaves of the pipal tree were shimmering beneath the overcast night sky just as if they were flashy earrings, and inside the girl was trembling and holding onto Randhir. Earlier, after reading each and every section of an English newspaper (even its ads) throughout the day, Randhir had gone out onto his balcony to relax a little as evening approached. The girl, probably a worker at the neighboring rope factory, was then standing under the tamarind tree to escape from the rain. Randhir had cleared his throat to get her attention and then signaled with his hand for her to come up.

He had been very lonesome for a number of days. On account of the war, almost all the Christian girls in Bombay, ones he was used to getting for cheap, had been conscripted into the Women's Auxiliary Forces. Many had opened "dancing" schools in the Fort where only British soldiers were allowed. Randhir was depressed. He could no longer get these Christian girls. Even though he was more cultured and attractive than the soldiers, he wasn't allowed into the Fort's whorehouses, simply because he wasn't white.

Before the war he had slept with many Christian girls, both in Nagpada and in the area around the Taj Hotel. He knew he was far more familiar with the intricacies of such relationships than the Christian boys with whom the girls pretended to be in love, only to lure one of these fools into marriage.

To be honest, Randhir had called the girl up just to have revenge upon Hazel for her new and arrogant indifference to him. Hazel lived in the apartment beneath his, and each morning she would put on her uniform, place her khaki hat crosswise over her military-style haircut, and come outside to strut off down the sidewalk as though she expected everyone in front of her to fall to the ground sacrificing their bodies to provide her with a carpet to walk across.

Randhir wondered why he was so obsessed with those Christian girls. Of course they were good at showing off all they had to show off, they talked about their periods without hesitating at all, they talked about their past love affairs, and they loved dance music so much that they started tapping their feet whenever they heard it. This is all true enough, and yet other women could be like that too.

When Randhir motioned for the girl to come up, he didn't imagine that he would go to bed with her. But when he saw her soaked clothes, he feared that she might catch pneumonia and so said, "Take those off. You'll catch cold."

She understood, and her eyes flashed with shame. When Randhir took off his white *dhoti* and offered it to her, she hesitated a moment and then unwrapped her dirty *kashta* sari, placed it to the side and quickly flung the dhoti over her lap. Then she began trying to remove her skin-tight bra that was tied together in a knot stuck between her cleavage.

She kept trying to loosen the knot with the aid of her nails but the rain had tightened it. When she got tired of this and admitted defeat, she turned to Randhir and said in Marathi, "What can I do? It's stuck."

Randhir went to sit by her and try his luck with the knot. After vainly trying for some time, he grabbed one edge of her bra's neckline in one hand, its other edge with his other hand, and yanked roughly. The knot broke. Her breasts sprung out, and for a moment he imagined himself a skillful potter who had shaped her breasts from finely kneaded clay.

Her breasts were firm and fresh like a potter's newly

turned vessels. A shade darker than tan, they were completely unblemished and imbued with a strange radiance: just beneath the skin there seemed to be a layer of faint light giving off a spectral glow like how a pond can radiate light from beneath its turgid surface.

✣

It was a monsoon day just like today. Outside the window the pipal tree's leaves were fluttering. The girl slept entwined with Randhir, and her rain-soaked clothes lay in a messy heap on the floor. The heat spreading from the girl's dirty naked body felt the same to Randhir as what he had experienced when bathing in the grimy, hot public baths during the dead of winter.

All night the two clung to each other as though they had become one. They must not have said more than a couple words, as what they had to communicate was accomplished by their breath, lips, and hands. All night Randhir caressed her breasts, arousing her small nipples and the nerves around her dark aureoles, and throughout the night tremors rippled up and down her body that were so strong that from time to time Randhir too quivered with delight.

Randhir knew all about such sensual pleasures. He had slept holding the breasts of countless girls. He had slept with girls so untrained that after cuddling up to him they would go on to talk about all the household things you shouldn't mention to a stranger. He had also slept with girls who did all the work so that he could just lie there. But this girl, this girl who had been trembling beneath the tamarind tree and whom he had called up to his room, she was very different.

All night her body emitted a strange smell at once alluring and repellent. With every breath, Randhir took in this ambivalent odor that came from everywhere—her armpits, her breasts, her hair, and her stomach. All night he told himself that he wouldn't have felt that close to her if her naked body hadn't smelled that way, if it didn't have that smell that entered into his every fiber and invaded his every thought.

For one night this odor united Randhir and the girl.

They became one, descending into an animal place where they existed only in pure pleasure, a place that despite being temporary was also eternal and that while being a sort of transcendent elation was also a quieted calm. They had become one, like a bird flying so high in the sky that it appears motionless.

This scent emanated from every pore of the girl's body. He recognized it but he couldn't describe it: it was like the pleasing aroma that dirt gives off after you sprinkle it with water. No, it wasn't like that at all. It was something different. It was without any of the artificiality of perfume but pure and real. It was as real and old as the story of men and women itself.

Randhir hated the smell of sweat. After bathing, he would normally sprinkle aromatic baby powder under his armpits and elsewhere or use some other substance to cover up the smell. So it was amazing that he kissed the girl's hairy armpits over and over and was not at all disgusted, but rather found this surprisingly pleasurable. Her delicate armpit hairs were damp from her sweat that gave off this scent at once evocative and yet unplaceable. Randhir felt like he knew this scent—it was familiar, he knew it in his bones, but he lacked the words to explain it to anyone.

## 2

It was a monsoon day just like today, exactly like today. When he looked through the window, he saw the leaves of the pipal tree trembling in the rain, rustling and fluttering in the breeze. It was dark and yet the night gave off a faint glow, as though the raindrops had stolen some of the stars' radiance. It was a monsoon day just like today back when Randhir had had only one teak bed in his room, though now there was another along with a dressing table consigned to a corner. It was a monsoon day just like today, the weather was just the same, with the same twinkling rain, and yet the sharp aroma of henna perfume hung in the air.

The second bed was empty. Randhir lay on his stomach, his head turned to look out the window at the leaves of the pipal tree quivering in the rain, and next to him a fair-skinned girl had fallen asleep after struggling unsuccessfully to cover herself with her naked limbs. Her red silk pants lay on the other bed, from which hung one knotted end of her pants' deep red drawstring. Her other clothes were strewn over the bed as well: her flowery *kameez*, her bra, underpants, and veil—and everything was red, bright red. And the clothes all smelled strongly of her henna perfume's pungent aroma.

Her black hair was flecked with glitter, and her face was covered with rouge and a sparkly makeup that dissolved together to produce a sick grayish hue. The poor girl! Her bra's badly dyed fabric had run and stained her pale breasts red in places.

Her breasts were the color of milk, white with a faint bluish tinge, and her armpits were badly shaven, leaving a grayish stubble. Over and over when Randhir looked at the girl, he felt as though he had just exhumed her from some box, as though she were a book or a porcelain vessel: just as ink spots may mar the cover of a book sent from the printer's, or as scratches appear on porcelain treated roughly during delivery, he found the very same marks on her body.

Earlier Randhir had untied the string fastening her bra, which had left deep lines on the tender flesh of her back and beneath her breasts. Her waist also bore the mark of her tight drawstring. Her necklace's heavy and sharp-edged jewels had left scratches across her chest that made it look as though she had torn at her skin with her nails.

It was a monsoon day just like today, the sound of the rain on the pipal tree's tender leaves exactly the same, and Randhir listened to it throughout the night. The weather was wonderful, and the breeze was pleasantly cool, but the overpowering aroma of henna perfume lay thick in the air.

Randhir continued to caress the girl's milky white breasts. His fingers felt ripples of pleasure run up and down her tender body and faint tremors coming from its deepest recesses. When Randhir pressed his chest against hers, he felt every nerve in his body vibrate in response to her passion. But something was missing: the attraction he had felt to the ghatin girl's scent, the pull more urgent than a baby crying for his mother's milk, that instinctual call surpassing all words.

Randhir looked through the iron bars on the window. Nearby the leaves of the pipal tree were fluttering, and yet he was looking beyond this at the distant overcast sky where the clouds cast an eerie glow that reminded him of the light of the ghatin girl's breasts.

A girl lay next to Randhir. Her body was as soft as dough made with milk and butter. The aromatic scent of henna rising from her sleeping body seemed to be fading little by little. Randhir could barely stand this poisonous, gut-wrenching odor: it smelled acidic, the strange type of acidity he associated with acid reflux—a sad scent, without color, without exhilaration.

Randhir looked at the girl lying by his side. Feminine charm touched her only in places, just as drops of spoilt milk fleck water. In truth Randhir still longed for the ghatin girl's natural scent—so much lighter and yet so much more penetrating than the scent of henna—the scent that was so welcome, that had excited Randhir exactly so naturally.

Trying for the last time, Randhir ran his hand over the girl's milky skin, but he felt nothing. Even though she was a respected judge's daughter, had graduated from college, and had hundreds of her male college classmates crazy about her, Randhir's new wife couldn't excite him. In the dying scent of henna, he tried to find the scent of the ghatin girl's dirty naked body that he had enjoyed when outside the window the leaves of the pipal tree had glistened in the rain, exactly like today.

---

Page 197, "The Fort" refers to that area of town that existed within Bombay's old city walls. Charles Boone, the British East India Company's Bombay Governor from 1715 to 1722, began their construction. They had twelve bastions with cannons, and three gates: Apollo Gate, to the southeast; Church Gate in the west; and Bazaar Gate to the north. Fort St. George constituted the easternmost extent of the wall, which remained standing until 1863.

Page 198, *kashta*: A sari that at nine yards is longer than average and that is wrapped in a special way—passed from the front between a woman's legs and tucked into the waist from behind—and associated with the underclass and with coarse eroticism.

# Translation

Carlito Azevedo | Translated by Sarah Rebecca Kersley from Portuguese (Brazil)

Brazilian poet and translator Carlito Azevedo was born in 1961 in Rio de Janeiro, where he still lives. In 1991, he won the Prêmio Jabuti, Brazil's most important literary prize, for his debut collection *Collapsus Linguae*. He followed this with three other collections, all met with accolades by the Brazilian press, and an anthology, now in its second edition. After a break of 13 years without publishing new work, Azevedo's brand new collection, *Monodrama*, was published at the end of 2009.

In addition to his own poetry, he has played a significant role in the poetry scene in Brazil via the review journal *Inimigo Rumor*, co-founded and edited by Azevedo. With twenty editions since 1997, the journal has become one of the best-known points of reference for emerging Brazilian poets, new translations into Portuguese, and essays and reviews of contemporary poetry.

English translations of Azevedo's work have previously appeared in *Nothing the Sun Could not Explain: 20 Contemporary Brazilian Poets* (Sun and Moon Press, 1997), and *Lies about the Truth: 14 Brazilian Poets*, in the journal *New American Writing* (2000), in which editor Régis Bonvicino presented Azevedo to US readers alongside other poets of the "new generation" in Brazil.

One of the delights in translating poetry is when

aspects inherent in the original text reveal themselves only in the translation. This was particularly true in this case. Creating an English version of the poem "Translation"—a nod to the Brazilian concrete movement of the 1950s—was a compelling challenge, calling for an interpretation of concept and a reproduction of visual form. To achieve the latter, the English had to contain the exact same number of characters as the original.

The original refers to two moons: one moon waxing and the other waning, and I interpreted the poem to be an evocation of the impalpable point at which the paths of these two moons cross. My translation exchanges moons for tides, evoking the point at which the path of an incoming tide crosses with that of an outgoing tide. The lunar notion of the original remains implicit in the translation (accentuated by the fact that the moon causes the tides). One of the most interesting things about translating this poem was the fact that the tidal notion of the original became apparent to me only after I had completed the translation, with the presence of the words IN and OUT in both the original and the translation.

Original text: Carlito Azevedo, from *Collapsus Linguae*. Rio de Janeiro: Editora LYNX, 1991.

# Traduzir

( d u a   s ( l i   n g ( u   a g e (<br>
n s d )   i f ) e   r ) e n   ) t e s<br>
( u m a   s ( o n   a n ( t   e & a (<br>
OUT)   r a ) a   u ) s e   ) n t e<br>
( l u a   m(IN   g u ( a   n t e (<br>
l u a )   c r ) e   s ) c e   ) n t e

# Translation

(two d(if fe(r ent(<br>
lan) gu)a g)es )one<br>
(voi c(ed th(e oth(<br>
era) bs)e n)tt )ide<br>
(com i(ng IN(a nda(<br>
tid) eg)o i)ng )OUT

# Two Zapotec Poems by Natalia Toledo

Translated by Clare Sullivan from Spanish (Mexico)
from translations by the author from Zapotec

Natalia Toledo (Juchitán, Oaxaca, 1967) writes poetry in her native Zapotec and then translates her own verse into Spanish. Though she now lives in Mexico City, her poetry revolves around her Zapotec childhood with particular emphasis on myths of origin and children's games. The sound of Zapotec, a tone language, lends an almost incantatory nature to her poems. The language, though, has roots unrelated to either Spanish or English, and to translate the sound of her poetry it was necessary to rely on her own gifts as a translator into Spanish and to reinforce language with the strength of her imagery.

Toledo's poems express longing for her people's traditional ties with nature. In the poems that begin "Fire is reborn" and "Seated in the shadows" she conflates her own body with the natural world. In beautiful and evocative imagery she celebrates the way her community has relied upon nature for survival and meaning.

Toledo fears losing her language and the traditions that accompany it. And her fears are not unfounded. When I spoke to a linguist from Juchitán he told me that children no longer play games like "Los hijos," a traditional Zapotec group game similar to hide-and-seek, but instead opt for solitary entertainment like Gameboys. They are also losing the linguistic tradition that bound them together, as young people less than 20 years of age are no longer very likely to be bilingual. When I translate Natalia Toledo's poetry, I lose her sound of course, but my hope is to enter deeply into the originals and to create interest in the language and culture that produced them.

Original text: Natalia Toledo, *Guie' yaase', Olivo negro.* Mexico City: Culturas Populares y el Consejo Nacional para la cultura y las Artes (Conaculta), 2005.

Cayache batee ladxidó' guidxilayú
ti bandaga yaa rasi íque laga'.
Bandá' stinne' lu tapa neza rizá
nayeche' riabirí guidilade'.
Ti le' nga ra lidxe'
ti bacuzaguí cahuinni biaani' galaa deche'.
batanaya' naca ti yaza
ne guirá ni rudiina' naa
rituee laa ne tini biina' guie' stinne'.

Zapotec

Spanish

Se reproduce el fuego en la tierra del mundo
una hoja tierna duerme sobre mis párpados
Mi sombra camina por cuatro veredas
feliz mi piel de hormigas se estremece.
Un jardín es mi casa
y poseo una luciérnaga en el dorso que me trasluce.
La palma de mi mano es una hoja
y a todo aquél que me saluda
tiño con la leche de mi tallo.

Fire is reborn on the soil of the earth
a tender leaf sleeps upon my eyelids
My shadow walks the four paths
content, my skin shivers with ants.
A garden is my house
and the firefly on my back makes me translucent.
The palm of my hand is a leaf
and I tint all that waves to me
with milk from my stalk.

Gurié xa'na' ti ba'canda'
naca deche'ti bacuela bigundu'.
Xilase richeza layú
sica ora riaba biní.
Yudé guidxilayú cayuni ti bidunu
ndaani' guielua'
candá' naxhi nisaguie,
ma chi guidaagu' guiba'.

Zapotec

Spanish

Sentada bajo una sombra
mi espalda es un totomostle vencido.
La tristeza abre surcos
como el suelo en que se siembra.
El polvo del mundo
se remolina dentro de mis ojos
aroma de lluvia,
a punto está de cerrarse el cielo.

Seated in the shadows
my back is a broken corn stalk.
Sadness opens furrows
like the land that we sow.
Dust of the earth
whirls within my eyes
scent of rain,
the sky is about to cloud over.

# Verily He Is Risen

Mikhail Shishkin | Translated by Marian Schwartz from Russian (Russia)

For "Verily He Is Risen," Mikhail Shishkin took an excerpt from his novel, *The Seizure of Izmail*, and fashioned it as a self-contained story. The novel, first published in *Znamia* (2000) and later in book form by Vagrius publishers (2006), won the Russian Booker Prize in 2000 and has been translated into French, Italian, Serbian, and Chinese. (Shishkin also won the National Bestseller Prize and the Russian Big Book Prize for his most recent novel, *Maidenhair.*)

"Verily He Is Risen" is set in the post-Soviet era and features intelligent and sympathetic main characters who are neither criminals nor bureaucrats and whose language is therefore standard. The narrator harks back to Soviet-speak when he hears a woman who might have been his schoolmate and recalls the realia of a Soviet schoolchild's life and the kind of verse they recite. The story's post-Soviet setting is thrown into relief by the narrator's memory of his Soviet childhood's Socialist Realist poetry and Party-dominated school activities. Shishkin's word choice is intriguingly specific—"crone" rather than "old woman," "submariner" rather than "sailor"—and you can practically smell the bums reeking of urine. Shishkin uses his stylistic virtuosity not as an end in itself but to make Russia real.

Perhaps the most difficult moment occurs toward the beginning, when the crone intones, "Willow white, lash to white, willow whip, lash to tears!" What strikes the reader immediately in the Russian (phonetically: "Vyérba byéla, byéy da byéla, vyérba khlyóst, byéy da slyós!") are the assonances, rhymes, and repeated "byela," first as a predicate adjective and then a noun, and the economy of expression. I tried to maintain these three elements, though at the expense of the original assonance's battering quality.

*The Seizure of Izmail* is a concatenation of stories connected by coincidences of landscape, ideas, and motifs, not the historically based novel its title would suggest. Shishkin is a virtuosic stylist who has been compared favorably with Joyce, Nabokov, and Calvino. As the setting jumps between eras, from the twentieth to the twenty-first century, so too does the language, which is rich with allusions and quotations.

It has been my experience that the finest, most enduring authors are the most compelling to translate. Shishkin, particularly in this story, is one of a handful of such writers it has been my privilege to work with. His texts present many puzzles and challenges, sometimes more than their share, but solutions seem always to exist and own a certain elegance.

Original text: Mikhail Shishkin, "Voistinu voskrese" from *Vziatie Izmaila*. Moscow: Vagrius, 2000.

# ВОИСТИНУ ВОСКРЕСЕ

А помнишь, Франческа, Пасху?

Сначала на остановке перед домом наша полоумная старушка-горбушка веткой вербы все норовила стегануть прохожих и приговаривала:

- Верба бела, бей до бела, верба хлест, бей до слез!

И нас с тобой тоже легонько стеганула и перекрестила.

В субботу мы целый день клеили обои в нашей комнате и вечером, уставшие, прилегли. Проснулись часов в одиннадцать - чуть не проспали. Выглянули в окно. Пасхальная ночь была теплая, звездная, но ветреная. С Пушки, как всегда, шел гул машин. Внизу, под нами было видно, как из казино напротив выходят люди и направляются напротив через дорогу в церковь.

Ты обвязала голову легким платком, и мы спустились на улицу.

Людей в храме было совсем немного. Сразу бросились в глаза наша горбушка, подпевавшая громче всех тонким дряблым голоском, и пара бомжей, у одного была вместо руки культя, а другой крестился черной от грязи щепотью. От них густо несло мочой. У самого алтаря сгрудились старухи, по привычке прижавшись друг к другу, как в очереди, хотя было полно места. Остальная публика была, кажется, вся из казино - крепыши-бодигарды в дорогих костюмах и банкирские жены в мехах и в коконах из духов. А может, киллеры и проститутки. Кто их разберет.

Мы стояли все вместе, держали свечки, обвернутые бумажкой, и молились, каждый о своем.

То и дело верещали мобильные телефоны....

# Verily He Is Risen

Remember Easter, Francesca?

First our half-demented old crone kept trying to lash passers-by with a pussy willow branch, muttering, "Willow white, lash to white, willow whip, lash to tears!"

She gave you and me a light lashing, too, and made the sign of the cross over us.

We spent the whole day Saturday pasting up wallpaper in our room and in the evening, exhausted, took a nap. We woke at about eleven—nearly overslept—and looked out the window. The Easter night was warm and starry but windy. The rumble of cars reached from Pushkin Square, as usual. Down below, we could see people coming out of the casino opposite and heading across the street to the church.

You wound a light scarf around your head and we went downstairs and outside.

There were very few people in the church. First to catch our eye was our crone, singing along above everyone else in her thin, flaccid little voice, and a couple of bums, one with a stump instead of an arm, and the other crossing himself with a grimy pinch. They reeked of urine. The old women were bunched up right by the altar, pressed up close out of habit, the way they did in line, though there was plenty of room. The rest of those in attendance all seemed to be from the casino: brawny bodyguards in expensive suits, and bankers' wives in furs and perfume cocoons. Maybe even killers and hookers, too. Who could tell?

We were all standing together, holding candles wrapped in paper, and saying prayers, each his own.

Once in a while a cell phone would go off.

Then Christ rose, and together we began to sing:

"Christ is risen from the dead, trampling down death by death, and on those in the tombs bestowing life."

And we lit our Easter candles off one another's. I lit my candle off an old woman's—the flame was reflected in her eyeglasses' lenses—and you off mine.

From time to time the priest would exclaim, "Christ is risen!"

And we would chorus in response, "Verily he is risen!"

And again we would hear phones ringing here and there.

Then all of us together—murderers and whores, crones and bums, old women, you and I—started walking around the church.

Occasionally a flame would blow out in the April wind and we would share the Paschal fire: old women and murderers, whores and bums. Someone handed around paper cups to everyone.

And so we circled the church holding little cups that glowed in the darkness. And all of a sudden, for just a moment, I had the weird feeling that all this had happened before, or rather, no, that we had been circling this way holding flickering lights forever, first along the street, then behind the church, past the old bakery yards and now I don't know what, some office or other, then past the printing press's fence, over boards laid across the mud, then past our garbage bin and back to the street, toward the stop, where an empty streetcar had in fact stopped and no one went in or out of the open doors. And so we circled, yesterday and the day before yesterday, singing, "Christ is risen from the dead," to the chirping of our cells, swathed in the thick fragrance of expensive perfume and sour urine, which no wind could lift from our stations of the cross, just as it could not extinguish the candles in our cups, and we are circling today and will be circling this way tomorrow, and the day after tomorrow, and always.

The procession returned to the church, and soon afterward the elegantly dressed public began to disperse.

Some went right back across the street to the casino, some to the nightclub at the Lenkom Theater, and some to the disco in the Rossia Cinema.

We stood there a little longer and then left as well. We wanted to take a walk, but the wind had driven up the clouds and it had started to drizzle.

We went home. It was dark in the lobby, as always. Usually I carried a small flashlight or flicked my lighter, but now our Paschal candles lit the steps for us.

Behind the elevator we heard the sighs, snoring, and scratching of the bums who had taken shelter there.

At home you started to make black crosses on the door lintel using the soot from your flame. I was surprised.

"What's this?"

Somewhere you'd read you could protect your home and loved ones from misfortune this way.

We walked around our empty nighttime apartment putting crosses of Paschal soot on all the windows and doors.

We didn't have *kulich*, or *paskha*, or eggs, so we broke our fast with *pelmeni* from a packet.

Then we went to bed and held each other close on our little sofa, and all around us the clumsily pasted wallpaper creaked as it separated from the wall.

That night, protected by crosses of smoke, we conceived our child.

In the morning Zinaida Vasilievna, my father's wife, phoned and said, "Oh, Misha, Christ is risen, but our sailor is dead."

Remember that funeral, Francesca? We didn't know whether to laugh or cry. At first we absolutely could not find the morgue and ran around in circles for half an hour past garages and garbage bins. We were nearly late. There already were Zinaida Vasilievna, my brother Sasha and his wife and children, some women, and an old man with an artificial leg who'd been drunk since morning and who introduced himself as my father's friend. I'd never seen him before in my life. He had put a galosh on his fake foot, and for some reason he had a sandal on his real one, though it was all wrong for the season.

A few little groups were crowded by the morgue entrance. The line moved slowly, even though they were bringing out the dead in carts quickly and kept trying to hurry up the mourners.

Zinaida Vasilievna told me how my father had died.

"He fell from the bed and shouted, 'Zina! Zina, I can't see anything! More light!'"

How odd that before dying that drunkard of a veteran submariner shouted the same thing as Goethe.

As far as I remember, my father had always said that when he died we should put him in his coffin in uniform. He had his naval uniform, which he'd had altered from time to time as his figure spread. Indeed, they brought us out a gray-haired sailor. Lately his whole body had shaken, but now my father had a pacific look with his arms folded on his chest, as if he had calmed down, as if it wasn't so easy to burn up, especially wearing his sailor's vest.

He drank so much, especially in his last years, that it was odd his organism had held out. All his submariner friends had drunk themselves into the grave a long time ago. The coffin was too small and his head wouldn't fit so it was pressing into the side, which forced his chin into his chest, and my father had a strange lively expression on his face, slightly offended, as if to say, so they couldn't even put me in a decent coffin?

Zinaida Vasilievna went to yell at them, but they started jabbing at the receipt, saying she'd ordered a 180 but you see he didn't fit a 180. A woman came out wearing a stained white coat and rubber gloves and started explaining that you always had to order extra because the dead stretched out.

"You mean you didn't know?"

Zinaida Vasilievna waved her hand; she didn't want to get into it.

"Do what you like! I don't have the strength for all this."

We had to go to the crematorium in Mitino. They gave us a bus splattered to the windows in mud. Sasha and I took the lid, to cover the coffin. There were already nails hammered into the lid, but I didn't notice right away, not until I saw that the lid didn't sit right, something was in the way. I looked—and a nail was poking straight into my father's crown. Something reddish blue was oozing through the torn skin and into his gray hair. We brought him uncovered.

You watched all this with dumb amazement, and the

longer it lasted the more amazement there was in your eyes. My father's pal with the prosthesis kept pestering you and saying something about shitocrats and kikes and about how we needed to run the blackasses out of Moscow.

While we were riding in the creaky, battered bus—holding tight to the seat so as not to go flying on a pothole, and bracing the coffin with my foot—something reminded me of how when I was a child my father and I used to ride our bikes to the Ilinsky Forest every August before school started. Again and again my father would ride ahead on his heavy trophy bike, and I would shout, "Papka, wait up!" and try to catch up to him on my Eaglet, bounding over the roots. There were pine trees all around so it was better to meander over the paths. Or you'd run across sand and your wheels would get stuck.

With my father the forest became an ordinary sun-combed park, but I was afraid to go there by myself after one time when I'd had to make off from a drunk soldier with a busted-up red face. He jumped out at me from the bushes.

"Hey, you little fucker! Stop!"

I shied away, nearly fell off my bicycle, and started pedaling for all I was worth.

The soldier ran after me, his boots pounding.

"Stop, you little bastard!"

I pedaled with all my might, but the wheels were hopping over roots, and I was afraid I was about to fall, but it was the soldier who tripped and fell, and my Eaglet carried me off.

There was a line in front of the crematorium, too, so we were stuck in the bus for another hour.

Finally, they got under way. In charge of it all was a stately lady wearing a quilted vest and mohair cap. I was struck by her voice, which immediately reminded me of Natasha Erofeyeva, a girl in my grade at school. She was the school's best at reciting the poem about the Soviet passport and "I've disliked the oval since a child and since a child have drawn an angle," and lots of other poems in that vein, and therefore she performed at all the Pioneer and later Komsomol assemblies, and they even gave her a trip to Camp Artek, and everyone envied Natasha, but no one else could recite poems the way she did. And now this lady with Natasha Erofeyeva's voice was showing us who should stand where and do what. After asking whether anyone was going to speak and seeing that no speeches were anticipated, she herself began saying something about Christ, the coming resurrection and immortality, in the same voice and with the same intonation as if it were the passport poem. I looked into her face, but I still couldn't tell whether or not it was she. After all, more than twenty years had passed. People change.

She crossed herself and said in parting that we needed to hold the deceased's foot so he wouldn't come in the night. Everyone exchanged looks, but this was said in the kind of voice that no one dared disobey. I was standing at one end of the coffin and wanted to grab my father by the boot, but he was barefoot under the cover. I held on to his doubled-up toes through the material.

When it was time to put the lid on the coffin, I bent the nail back as best I could so it wouldn't hurt my father.

Then the woman in charge—who, by the way, was also looking at me, so it probably was Natasha after all—crossed herself again and pushed a lever. The lever jammed, and she had to push harder on it a couple of times. Then Tchaikovsky started playing somewhere, with a crackling and a hiss, and my father's coffin started descending slowly into immortality, assuming Natasha wasn't lying.

From the crematorium everyone took the same bus to Strogino for the funeral meal. We rattled over the Ring Road for a long time. The direct exit to Strogino was being dug up so we had to wander around an extra half hour.

Everyone was well-shaken, tired, and famished. All we'd had was coffee early that morning, and it was already getting to be evening. We drove up to the building. A huge new never-ending building. I remember a cloud's shadow crawling across the wall: half the building in shadow, half in sun.

There were two elevators, the ordinary small one and one for furniture. We all jammed into the big one and, naturally, got stuck. How many of us were there? Ten or so. In short, everyone who had been at the funeral. The elevator tensed, jerked, went dark, and died.

We started pressing buttons, to no avail; we tried calling the dispatcher and got silence. We shouted but no one was in the lobby. We kicked the doors and called for help. I don't even know how long we stood there packed in so tightly we couldn't sit. The children started whining. Someone started laughing. Then everyone did—from exhaustion and nerves. We stood there, hanging in a dark box between floors, and laughed.

Zinaida Vasilievna said, "This must be Pavlusha having his revenge on us for that coffin!"

And everyone started laughing again.

Finally someone heard us. Some kid. He asked, "What should I do?"

"Call the dispatcher's office!"

And Sasha, my brother, shouted, "Forget the dispatcher! Bring an ax!"

So they opened the door somehow with the ax.

We walked up the stairs and sat down at the table. The neighbor ladies had set it for us a long time ago and had almost given up on us.

And you, Francesca, who before had always refused vodka, now asked for some.

We got back late, on nearly the last Metro train.

You were silent the whole way, put your head on my shoulder, and fell asleep, exhausted.

That was when, on the deafening night train, I think I first understood why we needed to come together like that. Why we needed just that gathering. That woman at the crematorium. That elevator. Here's why: it was beautiful. And for this reason and no other, we needed to hold on to the coffin with my father, who grew overnight, and that lady Charon with Natasha Erofeyeva's voice, and that elevator, that calling for an ax, because it was all—beautiful. Beautiful, Francesca, do you see?

While we were riding then, a beer can was rolling around on the floor. Heineken. Even now I can see it rolling, rattling emptily, to the end of the car, where some old lady was asleep, stretched out on a bench, wearing felt boots, galoshes, and a quilted jacket, resting her head on an Adidas bag. This old woman was beautiful, too.

Shortly before his death, my father suddenly wanted

to have his photograph taken with me.

I said, "What for?"

He tried to talk me into it.

"I'm going to croak, Mishka, and you can look at the photo and maybe remember your sailor-father!"

Then I said, just to get him to back off, "Fine, let's go, sailor-father!"

We went to the studio next to their building right by the exit to Strogino. We sat down in front of a camera that dated to the Lumière Brothers. The photographer, a young girl with a boyish haircut, said, removing her gum with her fingers, "I wish you'd smile!"

The smile must not have worked out very well for us because the girl burst out laughing.

"Well then, say 'cheese'!"

Not that long ago I was searching for something, sorting through old papers, and all of a sudden I looked—and it was that photograph. My father and I are sitting, earlobes touching, each with a mouth full of cheese.

# Prefaced by Blood

H. E. Sayeh | Translated by Fayre Makeig from Persian (Iran)

Hushang Ebtehaj (pen name, H. E. Sayeh, "shadow") was born in 1928 in Rasht, Iran. After the publication of his first book, the young poet joined Tehran's literary community, burgeoning since World War II had loosened the shah's hold on the nation. But hope proved short-lived. Helped by the CIA and British operatives, the shah's grasp tightened in the early 1950s. Many poets and scholars were imprisoned or killed, but Sayeh stayed true to his social conscience and continued his literary activities.

It is difficult to understand or appreciate Sayeh's work outside the thousand-year tradition of Persian poetry. Yet the pleasure of trying to translate Persian poetry into English is, in fact, its interweave. Pull any one thread, and you will immediately meet the resistance of the closest knots. And so you must follow one thread, and then another to make sense of the first. In the case of Sayeh, the closest knots are the classical poet Hafiz, the father of modern poetry, Nima Yushij (1896–1960), and the politics of resistance.

Both in Sayeh's masterful ghazals and in his carefully crafted free verse, one hears a sensitivity to sound and syntax informed by a lifetime reading Hafiz. This study culminated in *Hafiz, by Sayeh*, a close-reading analysis of Hafiz's divan, published in 1994.

Then there is Sayeh's mentor, Nima Yushij. Most major modern poets—Ahmad Shamlu, Forugh Farrokhzad,

Mehdi Akhavan Saless, Sohrab Sepehri—use Yushij's work as a starting point. Not only did Yushij break with tradition by writing in free verse, but he also introduced new meanings to old metaphors: Night, once a time to wait for the beloved, now symbolized political repression. "Color" is slang for the shah's secret police. A nightingale is an activist who refuses to be silenced. The dawn promises freedom from oppression.

"Prefaced by Blood" was written in the early 1980s, soon after Sayeh was released from a year-long prison sentence. After a lifetime of quiet opposition to the shah's regime, to be persecuted by the Ayatollah Khomeini and to see his friends killed was a shock. The poem chronicles a history of slain heroes, from the 8th-century revolutionary Babak Khorramdin and the 9th-century Sufi heretic al-Hallaj (crucified for saying "I and the Truth are one"), to the anticolonial leaders Patrice Lumumba, Che Guevara, and Morteza Keivan (executed at the shah's behest in the early 1950s), to the residents of the southern province of Khuzistan (in which Sayeh names three devastated towns) and an unnamed boy killed in the Iran-Iraq War.

Though in this poem and others Sayeh shares the themes and influences of dozens of contemporary Persian poets, his work will pass the test of generations. It combines a classically informed poetic sensitivity with a conscience and vision unique, I think, to the brave poets of Iran. Every poem is a gem, set by a master poet of our time.

Original text: H. E. Sayeh, *Tasian*. Tehran: Karnameh Publishing, 2006.

# دیباچهٔ خون

نه، هراسی نیست
من هزاران بار
تیر باران شده ام
و هزاران بار
دلِ زیبای مرا از دار آویخته اند
و هزاران بار
با شهیدانِ تمامِ تاریخ
خونِ جوشانِ مرا
به زمین ریخته اند.

سر گذشتِ دلِ من
زندگی نامهٔ انسان است
که لبش دوخته اند
زنده اش سوخته اند
و به دارش زده اند.

# Prefaced by Blood

No, I am not afraid.
I have been shot
thousands of times.
And thousands of times
my beautiful heart
has been strung on a noose,
my blood spilled
warm on the ground:
the millennia of martyrs.

My heart chronicles
the accounts of one whose
lips have been sewn,
life-force turned to ash,
body pinned to a cross.

آه ای بابکِ خرّم دین
تو لومومبا را می دیدی
و لومومبا می دید
مرگِ خونینِ مرا در بولیوی
رازِ سر سبزیِ حلاج این است:
ریشه در خون شُستن
باز از خون رُستن.

در ویتنام هزاران بار
زیرِ تیغِ جلاد
زخم برداشته ام
وندر آن آتش و خون
باز چون پرچمِ فتح
قامت افراشته ام.

آه، ای آزادی
دیر گاهی ست که از اندونزی تا شیلی
خاکِ این دشتِ جگر سوخته با خونِ تو می آمیزد
دیرگاهی ست که از پیکرِ مجروحِ فلسطین شب و روز

Oh, Babak Khorramdin—
you foresaw Lumumba
and Lumumba foresaw
my bloody death in Bolivia.
The secret of the evergreen Hallaj
is this: roots washed in blood
shall put forth again in blood.

In Vietnam I was cut
thousands of times
by the executioner's blade,
and again I rose
in fire and blood
like a banner of victory.

Ah, liberty—
from Indonesia to Chile,
the dust of these tormented plains
has long been mixed with your blood.

خون فرو می ریزد
و هنوز از لبنان
دود بر می خیزد.

سال ها پیش، مرا با کیوان کُشتند
شاه هر روز مرا می کُشت
و هنوز
دستِ شاهانه دراز است پیِ کشتنِ من
هم از آن دستِ پلید است که در خوزستان
در هویزه، بستان، سوسنگرد
این چنین در خون آغشته شدم
و همین امروز
با مسلمانِ جوانی که خطِ پشتِ لبش
تازه سبزی می زد کشته شدم.

نه، هراسی نیست
خونِ ما راهِ درازِ بشریت را گُلگون کرده ست
دستِ تاریخ، ظفر نامهٔ انسان را
زیبِ دیباچهٔ خون کرده ست.

Blood pours from the wounded body of Palestine
day and night, and even now,
from Lebanon, smoke is rising.

Years back, I was killed alongside Keivan.
The shah killed me every day
and even now
an imperial hand stretches forth,
pointing me out for death—
the same defiled hand
that smeared me with blood
in Khuzistan, in Hoveizeh, Bostan, Susangard—
and again today
I was killed beside a Muslim boy,
his mustache just about to grow.

No, I am not afraid.
Our blood adorns humanity's long road—
the chronicles of every human triumph
are prefaced by blood.

آری، از مرگ هراسی نیست
مرگِ در میدان این آرزوی هر مرد است
من دلم  از دشمنْ کام شدن می سوزد
مرگِ با دشنهٔ دوست؟
دوستان!  این  درد است.

نه، هراسی نیست
پیش ما ساده ترین مسئله ای مرگ است
مرگِ ما سهل تر از کَندنِ یک برگ است
من به این باغ می اندیشم
که یکی پشتِ درش با تبری تیز کمین کرده ست.

دوستان گوش کنید
مرگِ من مرگِ شماست
مگذارید شما را بکُشند
مگذارید که من بارِ دگر
در شما کُشته شوم.

It is not death I fear.
To die on the battlefield is noble,
and I too seethe when an enemy wins.
But death at the hand of a friend?
This, friends, is anguish.

No, I am not afraid.
Death is the simplest problem in our path—
it is easier to die than to pluck a leaf.
But I fear for this garden
where just outside the gate
someone waits in ambush
with a sharpened axe.

Listen, friends:
your death is mine.
Do not let them kill me.
Do not let me die in you again.

# Translation is a Testing Ground

Roberto Bolaño | Translated by Natasha Wimmer from Spanish (Chile)

This piece was probably written sometime during the last year of Roberto Bolaño's life, and was published in late 2002 or early 2003 in the Chilean newspaper *Las Últimas Noticias*. Bolaño was a regular columnist for *Las Últimas Noticias*, and around this time he wrote to his editor, Andrés Braithwaite, to apologize for the delay in sending in a column: "I've had it up to here with all the tests. And now I'm on the transplant list. In other words, they could call me at any minute, since my blood group—B+—is rare, and according to the doctors, I'm not in a position to chivalrously give up my place in line. You know what this means. More Bolaño or *finis terrae* or *c'est tout*. I'm sorry to make things difficult for you, but ultimately that's what editors are there for."

Bolaño's email exchange with Braithwaite is quoted by Ignacio Echevarría in his notes to an edition of Bolaño's collected essays and journalism, *Between Parentheses*, soon to be published in the United States by New Directions. Almost all of the pieces were written in the last five years of his life, and they vibrate with the exuberance of his rapid rise to literary stardom and the urgency of his quest to write as much as he could before ill health overtook him.

"Translation Is a Testing Ground" is possibly the only

piece Bolaño ever wrote about translation, and while it may not be particularly complimentary to translators, it eloquently describes the power of great literature to thrive in good, mediocre, or outright bad translation. The last paragraph is one of the most beautiful passages of Bolaño's nonfiction, and also one of the most challenging for the translator, because of its incantatory rhythm and its mixture of informal exhortation and exquisite formal imagery.

Original text: Roberto Bolaño, *Entre Parentesis*. Barcelona: Anagrama, 2004.

# La traducción es un yunque

¿Qué es lo que hace que un autor tan apreciado por quienes hablamos español sea un autor de segunda o tercera fila, cuando no un absoluto desconocido, entre quienes se comunican en otras lenguas? El caso de Quevedo, recordaba Borges, tal vez sea el más flagrante. ¿Por qué Quevedo no es un poeta vivo, es decir digno de relecturas y reinterpretaciones y ramificaciones, en ámbitos foráneos a la lengua española? Lo que lleva directamente a otra pregunta: ¿por qué consideramos nosotros a Quevedo nuestro más alto poeta? ¿O por qué Quevedo y Góngora son nuestros dos más altos poetas?

Cervantes, que en vida fue menospreciado y tenido por menos, es nuestro más alto novelista. Sobre esto no hay casi discusión. También es el más alto novelista, según algunos el inventor de la novela, en tierras donde no se habla español y donde la obra de Cervantes se conoce, sobre todo, gracias a traducciones. Estas traducciones pueden ser buenas o pueden no serlo, lo que no es óbice para que la razón del Quijote se imponga o impregne la imaginación de miles de lectores, a quienes no les importa ni el lujo verbal ni el ritmo ni la fuerza de la prosodia cervantina que obviamente cualquier traducción, por buena que sea, desdibuja o disuelve.

Sterne le debe mucho a Cervantes y en el siglo XIX, el siglo novelístico por excelencia, también Dickens. Ninguno de los dos, es casi una obviedad decirlo, sabía español, por lo que se deduce que leyeron las aventuras del *Quijote* en inglés. Lo portentoso -y sin embargo natural en este caso- es que esas traducciones, buenas o no, supieron transmitir lo que en el caso de Quevedo o de Góngora no supieron ni probablemente jamás sabrán: aquello que distingue una obra maestra absoluta de una obra maestra ...

# Translation is a Testing Ground

What is it that makes an author, so beloved by those of us who speak Spanish, a figure of the second or third rank, if not an absolute unknown, among those who speak other languages? The case of Quevedo, as Borges reminds us, is perhaps the most flagrant. Why isn't Quevedo a living poet, by which I mean a poet worthy of being reread and reinterpreted and imitated in spheres outside of Spanish literature? Which leads directly to another question: why do we ourselves consider Quevedo to be our greatest poet? Or why are Quevedo and Góngora our two greatest poets?

Cervantes, who in his lifetime was disparaged and looked down upon, is our greatest novelist. Regarding this there is almost no debate. He's also the greatest novelist—and according to some, the inventor of the novel—in lands where Spanish isn't spoken and where the work of Cervantes can for the most part only be read in translation. The various translations may be good or they may not be, which hasn't prevented the essence of *Don Quixote* from being imprinted on or filtered into the imagination of thousands of readers, who don't care about the verbal riches or the rhythm or force of Cervantine prose, a prose that any translation, no matter how good, obviously distorts or dissolves.

Sterne owes much to Cervantes, and in the 19th century—the century of the novel par excellence—so does Dickens. Neither of the two, it almost goes without saying, spoke Spanish, by which one can deduce that they read the adventures of *Don Quixote* in English. The wonderful thing—and yet also the natural thing, in this case—is that those translations of *Don Quixote*, good or not, were able to convey what, in the case of Quevedo or Góngora, wasn't conveyable and probably never will be: the quality that distinguishes an absolute masterpiece from an ordinary masterpiece, or, if such a thing exists, the quality that distinguishes a living literature, a literature that belongs to all mankind, from a literature that's only the heritage of a certain tribe or a part of a certain tribe.

Borges, who wrote absolute masterpieces, explained it once already. Here's the story: Borges goes to the theater to see a production of *Macbeth*. The translation is terrible, the production is terrible, the actors are terrible, the staging is terrible. Even the seats are uncomfortable. And yet when the lights go down and the play begins, the spectators, Borges among them, are immersed once again in the fate of characters who traverse time, shivering once again at what we can call magic, for lack of a better word.

Something similar happens with the popular Passion plays, in which the eager amateur actors who once a year stage the crucifixion of Christ manage—on the wings of divine mystery—to transcend the most dreadful absurdity or unconscious heresy, though perhaps it isn't actually divine mystery but art.

How to recognize a work of art? How to separate it, even if just for a moment, from its critical apparatus, its exegetes, its tireless plagiarizers, its belittlers, its final lonely fate? Easy. Let it be translated. Let its translator be far from brilliant. Rip pages from it at random. Leave it lying in an attic. If after all of this a kid comes along and reads it, and after reading it makes it his own, and is faithful to it (or unfaithful, whichever) and reinterprets it and accompanies it on its voyage to the edge, and both are enriched and the kid adds an ounce of value to its original value, then we have something before us, a machine or a book, capable of speaking to all human beings: not a plowed field but a mountain, not the image of a dark forest but the dark forest, not a flock of birds but the Nightingale.

FOCUS ON UYGHUR POETRY

# Focus on Uyghur Poetry

Edited and Translated by Dolkun Kamberi and Jeffrey Yang

The Uyghurs are an ancient people whose forebears are thought to be Turk-Tocharian, and have lived in Central Asia since the first millennium BCE. This area has played an important role since early times because of its favorable geographic location on the ancient trade routes between the East and the West, connecting Greco-Roman civilization with Indian Buddhist culture and Central and East Asian traditions. Burgeoning commerce and cultural exchange brought a cosmopolitan character to the region, marked by linguistic, racial, and religious tolerance.

Over hundreds of years, the Uyghurs have developed a unique culture and have made significant contributions in the history, literature, sciences, architecture, music, song, dance, crafts, and fine arts of Central Eurasian civilization. Most of the ten million Uyghurs today live in the Uyghur Autonomous Region that comprises roughly one-sixth of China's territory, though diasporic Uyghur communities have settled all around the world. Uyghur religious beliefs are a mix of Shamanism, Buddhism, Manichaeism, Nestorianism, and Islam, which was adopted as the official religion in 960 CE, during the rule of King Sultan Satuq Bughra Khan.

The word Uyghur (also transliterated as Uighur or Uygur) means "unity" with undercurrents of "union," "coalition," and "federation." The name's earliest known appearance can be traced to the Orkhon Göktürk inscriptions carved on stone monuments in Central Mongolia, and can be found in medieval Uyghur, Manichaean, and Sogdian scripts, as well as Arabic-Persian scripts. Apart from these Inner/Central Asian designations, the name appears in diverse Chinese manuscripts throughout history, where it has been transliterated into more than one hundred forms: Die, Chidie, Hu, Saka/Scythian, Hun, Uysun, Dingling, Qangqil, Sogdian, Tokharian, Hugu, Huihe, Yuanhe, and on.

The Orkhon Göktürk inscriptions, also known as the Orkhon-Yenisey inscriptions, were discovered in the late nineteenth century by a Russian archaeologist in the Orkhon Valley near the Yenisey River. They are the earliest example of writing in any Turkic language—the runiform text telling the story of Turkic reconstruction after many years of Chinese subjugation. The inscriptions are dated to the early eighth century, and the runiform is thought to be an early form of Old Uyghur, also called Old Turkic (or Türki), once the lingua franca of Central Asia. The Orkhon-Yenisey alphabet was eventually replaced by the cursive form of the Sogdian (early Persian) script, and the Uyghur language continued to transform as it became the literary language of many Turkic peoples, spreading widely during the Iduqut (holy chieftain) Uyghur Khanate from the mid-eighth to ninth centuries and the Karakhanid Khanate from the ninth to thirteenth centuries, and through the Chagatay Khanate into the late seventeenth century. Modern Uyghur belongs to the Ural-Altaic language family, and is related to Uzbek, Kazakh, Azerbaijan, Turkmen, and Kyrgyz. Although at least seven different writing systems of the language have been created, an Arabic-based alphabet is most common today, with a Cyrillic and two Latin scripts also in use. In other words, in the land of the Uyghurs, we are not only in the realm of chickens trying to talk to ducks, as the Cantonese humorously say in regard to the Han Chinese, but of chickens trying to write to ducks.

As with all civilizations that have depended on a highly developed oral culture to pass down their literature, customs, myths, and beliefs through the generations, the literary art with the longest and richest tradition for the Uyghurs is poetry—a poetry rooted in song and music. For many centuries, Uyghur poetry was written in Persian, and poets such as Lutfi (c. 1367-1463) and Ali-Shir Nava'i (1441-1501), excelled in ghazal and rubai forms, as well as masnavi rhymed couplets, qasida, and dörtlük, tuyugh quatrains, which retain a similar *aaba* rhyme scheme as the rubai, but all the rhyming words are homonyms and the meter is based on the syllabics of Turkish folk music, rather than a Persian-Arabic form.

One of the most famous Uyghur texts is Mahmud al-Kashgari's eleventh-century Turkic-Arabic Dictionary of the Turk Languages (*Diwan Lughat al-Turk*), which is less Webster's than an encyclopedic lexicography and ethnography of Turkish culture, dedicated to the Abbasid Caliph al-Muqtadi, and, among other things, includes maps and poetry: elegies, heroic songs, drinking and hunting songs, love lyrics, debates, nature and gnomic poems. We've included translations of a few of these poems, as well as some fragments of early medieval Uyghur Buddhist and Manichean poems unearthed in the Turpan Basin.

We've also included a few poems by the famous

modern Uyghur poets Abdurehim Ötkür and Abduhalik Uyghur, as well as a recent poem, "Motherland Shines My Heart" by Dilber Keyim Kizi. It is interesting to note that Kizi's poem was written in direct conversation (or subversion) with one of the most well-known Uyghur poems in recent memory, Teyipjan Eliyev's "Ode to the Motherland," which can be found in the standard, state-controlled Uyghur textbooks of the post-Mao era. Eliyev's poem opens, "China is my dear mother, the place of my birth, I am her son...." One must consider that if a Uyghur poet doesn't write like this, the risk of arrest and execution has proven to be high. Just looking over the names of Uyghur writers of the twentieth century, one can see that few have reached the fullness of their years; many were imprisoned and killed by their thirties.

"Every language," writes the Senegalese poet Léopold Senghor, "can provide material for the humanities, because every civilization is the expression, with its own peculiar emphasis, of certain characteristics of humanity." We hope to share a little of the depth and diversity of Uyghur poetry, writing that is evidence of a vibrant, evolving culture and civilization. Contemporary Uyghur poets such as Adil Tuniyaz, who has written many poems about beer, Polat Hewizulla, and Ahmatjan Osman are familiar with the work of the Russian modernists, Tartar futurists, French symbolists, western and eastern threads that converge, once again as in ancient times, at the Uyghur center. Who is listening? Osman, in his poem titled "Robinson Crusoe," gives us these lines, translated by scholar Michael Friederich: "I have to leave / To chain the world into my questions. / I will show all things / Through eyes of doubt. / I am the Robinson of this time, / I will build / My island / In another world."

# Three Poems by Abdurehim Ötkür

Abdurehim Ötkür (1923-1995) was born in Qumul, Uyghurstan. He is one of the most prominent contemporary Uyghur poets and scholars. Ötkür graduated from Uyghurstan College (now Xinjiang University) in 1942, and worked as a teacher, newspaper editor, and interpreter.

In 1940, Ötkür began to write poetry, and became actively involved with the Uyghur independence movement. In 1947, with other Uyghur writers, he traveled to Nanjing to advocate for Uyghur self-determination and independence. Ötkür was imprisoned twice by Chinese Communist authorities, once in 1952 and again in 1964, when he served a twelve-year sentence.

After his release, he worked as a carpenter for a few years until he was hired as the Deputy Director of the Literary Institute of the Xinjiang Academy of Social Sciences. He has published two poetry collections and two novels, one of which, *Trace*, is an expansion of his poem of the same name.

# ئىز

ياش ئىدۇق مۈشكۈل سەپەرگە ئاتلىنىپ ماڭغاندا بىز،
ئەمدى ئاتقا مىنگۈدەك بولۇپ قالدى ئەنە نەۋرىمىز.
ئاز ئىدۇق مۈشكۈل سەپەرگە ئاتلىنىپ چىققاندا بىز،
ئەمدى چوڭ كارۋان ئاتالدۇق، قالدۇرۇپ چۆللەردە ئىز.
قالدى ئىز چۆللەر ئارا، گايى داۋانلاردا يەنە،
قالدى ـنى نى ئارسلانلار دەشت چۆلدە قەبرىسىز.
قەبرىسىز قالدى دېمەڭ يۇلغۇن قىزارغان دالىدا،
گۈل ـ چېچەككە پۈركىنۈر تاڭدا باھاردا قەبرىمىز.
قالدى ئىز، قالدى مەنزىل، قالدى يىراقتا ھەممىسى،
چىقسا بوران، كۆچسە قۇملار، ھەم كۆمۈلمەس ئىزىمىز.
توختىماس كارۋان يولىدا گەرچە ئاتلار بەك ئورۇق،
تاپقۇسى ھېچ بولمىسا، بۇ ئىزنى بىزنىڭ نەۋرىمىز، يا چەۋرىمىز.

# Trace

We were young when we made the long journey on horseback
And now it is our grandchildren who have mounted the way
So few we were on our difficult journey, so young,
A trace left in the desert, we emerged a great caravan
The trace still remains in the desert, in the mountain passes,
Those Arslan-hearted ones, lions forgotten in the plains
In the deserts, without epitaphs without graves
In the field where the tamarisk turns red, don't say *left without graves,*
For our graves wrap themselves in blooms, flower at dawn in the spring
The trace lingered, the halting place lingered, they all linger far away
A storm rises, the dunes shift, winds pass, our trace will be as it was unburied
Endless caravan on the open road, horses tire and thirst,
But this trace will surely be found one day, by our children,
our grandchildren, no matter the time nor distant place

# خەجلە، خائىنلار خەجلە

خەجلە، خائىنلار، خەجلە، بۇ ئەلنىڭ مالىنى خەجلە،
يېتىشمەي قالسا گەر ئۇ، ھەم ئېلىپ سەن جانىنى خەجلە.

خېنىمغا ئۇسما دەپ خەجلە، بېگىمگە تاسما دەپ خەجلە،
ـتالانتاراجدىن قالغان پارچە نانىنى ھەم خەجلە.

دېھقانغا ئاچقۇزۇپ بوزنى، دۇكانغا توقۇتۇپ بۆزنى،
سېلىپ ئالۋاننى يۈز قاتلام، ئىچىپ سەن قاننى خەجلە.

كۆلدە بېلىقى كۆپ دەپ، يەر ئاستى بايلىقى كۆپ دەپ،
قەدەمدە مىڭ تېپىپ خەجلە، ئېچىپ سەن كاننى خەجلە.

پالانى ـئاقچىدۇركۆكچى، بۇ ئۆتكۈرمۇ يامان دوقچى،
دەپ پارچىلاپ بۇ مىللەتنى، سېتىپ ۋىجدانىنى خەجلە.

# Sell, Betrayers, and Spend

Sell, betrayers, sell, spend the State's properties
If that is not enough, take precious life to sell

Spend it on ladies' makeup; spend it on men's belts
After ruining everything, sell the last of the poor's food

Let peasants till polluted land; store the harvest in your vaults
Increase taxes 100%, suck people's blood, spend

We have enough fish in the lakes, rich natural deposits
Spoil the water, unearth the resources, sell, and spend

Accuse others and Ötkür as bad troublemakers
Divide the nation, sell your heart, and spend

JANUARY 8, 1949

# مەن ئاق بايراق ئەمەس

كۈمۈش كەبى يالتىراق، مەرۋايىتتەك پارقىراق،
بىر چوققا بار ئاسمانغا مەغرۇر بېشى تاقاشقان،
ئۇنىڭ ئېتى خانتەڭرى، تەڭرى تاغقا جايلاشقان.
مەشرىقتىن چىقسا ئاپتاپ، ھەممىدىن ئاۋال باشلاپ،
شۇ چوققىنى سۆيىدۇ، مەڭزىگە يېقىپ مەڭزىن،
ئۆتۈپ ئۇنىڭ قېشىدىن، غەرىبكە ماڭار ئاندىن.
كېچە بولسا تولۇن ئاي، ئۆتمەيدۇ ئۇندا قونماي،
يەتتە يۇلتۇز ھەم مۆكەر، زۇھەل بىلەن مۇشتەرى،
يوقلاپ ئۆتىدۇ ئۇنى، تازىم قىلىپ ھەر بىرى.
ئېرىمەيدۇ قىش يېزى، ئاق سايىدەك قار مۇزى،

كۆك بىكىگە تاقاقلىق، تەبىئەتنىڭ ئەركىسى،
تاشنى يېرىپ چىققان ئۇ، مۆجىزە ـ قار لەيلىسى.
شۇڭلاشقىمۇ بۇ چوققا، كۆرىنىدۇ كۆزلەرگە،
ئوت ئېچىلغان گۈل كەبى،
ياكى باھار كۈنلىرى، ئاققۇ قونغان كۆل كەبى،

# I Am Not a White Flag

Khan Tengri is a heavenly mountain
With a peak that reaches through the sky, shines
Like silver and pearls, so proud
The sun rises from the East, kisses the mountain,
Cheek against cheek, passes along
And travels West, away from the peak
On a full moon, the Seven Stars, Mercury,
Saturn, and Jupiter descend for a visit,
And before parting, bow to the mountain
White riverbeds of ice, the snow never melts,
Summer, winter, nature beats in his chest, breaks
Through the stones: a miracle snow orchid grows
The peak is a beautiful white flower,
On a spring day, a swan on a lake
The man from afar doesn't know
Such strength, says it is the flag of surrender

بۇنى بىلمەي بىر جاناب، خانتەڭرىگە بىر قاراپ،
دەپ تاشلىدى ـ " بۇ چوققا، ئېراقتىن قارىماققا،
ئوخشايدىكەن ئەل بولغان قوشۇن تۇتقان "بايراققا.
خانتەڭرى بۇنى ئاڭلاپ، كۈلۈۋەتتى قاقاقلاپ.
دېدى ـ " نەدە چوڭ بولغان بېشى قاپاق جانابسىز؟
قۇلاق سېلىڭ قالمىغاي بۇ گېپىڭىز جاۋابسىز.
دەرۋەقە ئاق مەن ئۈزۈم، ساقال، چېچىم ھەم يۈزۈم،
لېكىن ھەرگىز ئەمەسمەن سىز ئېيتقاندەك ئاق بايراق،
ـتەبىئىتىممىجەزىم ئاق بايراقتىن بەك يىراق.
ئادەم ئاتا ھەم ھاۋا، جەننەتتىن چىققان چاغدا،
تۇنجى تۇغۇلغان ئوغلى مەن ئىدىم بۇ زېمىندە،
بوز ئېچىپ، ئۇرۇق چاچقان يېشىل ۋادا تارىمدە.
ماھىم كېمىسى توپاندا، يول تاپالماي ئازغاندا،
ئاغزىمغا زەيتۇن چىشلەپ بارغان كەپتەر مەن ئىدىم،
ھاياتلىقنىڭ نىشانى ئاشۇ خەۋەر مەن ئىدىم.
قوش مۈڭگۈزلۈك ئىسكەندەر، باشلاپ كەلگەندە خەتەر،
ئۇنىڭ ئۆتەر يولىنى توساپ قويغان مەن ئىدىم.
يىپەك يۇدىگەن كارۋان قوڭغۇراق جاراڭلاتقان،
ئەشۇ قەدىم يوللاردا ھەم قورۇقچى پاسىۋان،

Khan Tengri hears this, laughs loudly and says,
"Where are you from? Listen, ignorant man,
Beyond question, I am not a white flag
My beard may be white, my hair, my face,
White, though make no mistake, I
Am not a white flag
I am the firstborn child of Adam and Eve
I am both Heaven and Earth
When Noah floundered in the flood without hope,
I was the dove he released, returning with the olive twig
When double-horned Alexander brought violence
To the land, it was I who blocked his path
Trade caravans on the Silk Road, bells chiming faintly,
There I was beside them, their guardian along history
For I completed the words in the Book of History,
Unknotting the many, so many, mysteries of the past
Paper, compass, printing, and the wonder
Of gun powder, passing through me, expanding
The world's moment
I rocked the cradle of civilization since time began
I have been here, from all-knowing Earth's prime

ـئاشتۇز بېرىپ كارۋانغا ھەم بولغانىدىم ساھىبخان.
ئەي جانابى مۇھتەرەم، بىلىپ قويۇڭ شۇنى ھەم،
تارىخ دېگەن كىتابىنىڭ خېتى مەندە پۈتۈلگەن،
ـنى نى چىگىش تۈگۈنلەر مېنىڭ بىلەن يېشىلگەن.
قەغەز، كومپاس، مەتبەئە، دورا دېگەن مۆجىزە،
مەندىن ئۆتۈپ جاھانغا تارالغان ھەم كېڭەيگەن.
مەدەنىيەت بۆشۈكىنى ئۆز قولۇمدا تەۋرەتكەن،
دېمەك تا ئەلمىساقتىن، بىلىم بار ھەم ئۇزاقتىن،
شۇڭا بېشىم ئاقارغان ھەتتا كىيگەن تونۇم ئاق،
لېكىن ئۆزۈم ئەمەسمەن سىز ئېيتقاندەك ئاق بايراق.
بۇ كەڭ زېمىن ۋەتىنىم، ئالما باغلىق جان ـ تېنىم،
ـچاچساقالنىڭ ئاقلىغى ـتارىخئەسرنىڭ ئۇلى،
كۆككە تاقاشقان بېشىم شۇ ۋەتەنىنىڭ سىمۋولى.
قارا بۇلۇت توسسىمۇ، چاقماق كېلىپ سوقسىمۇ،
ئېگىلمەستىن بۇ بېشىم، مەغرۇر تۇرار ھەممە ۋاق،
قانداق قىلىپ مەن ئەمدى بولۇپ قالاي ئاق بايراق؟!
قەلبىم قىزىل چوغدۇر، قىزىل تۇغنى كۆتۈرۈپ،
كېتىۋاتسام مەردانە، ناخشام غالىپ ياڭراق،
قايسى يۈزىڭىز بىلەن مېنى دەيسىز ئاق بايراق؟ "...

Moment and so my head is as white as my coat, but a white
Flag I will never become, no matter what you do
O great motherland, on which my life depends wholly,
Whiteness of hair and beard, the foundation of history
Peak reaching through sky the sign of the mother-
Land, if clouds obstruct or lightning strikes, still
I will stand firmly
My head doesn't bend; I do not sway
How, then, did I become a white flag to you?
My heart is red fire; I lift a blue flag with dignity;
I march boldly in ancientness, singing
My song of victory that echoes the world
You, have you forgotten the centuries,
The years of my sustenance, collecting
My treasures, that you in shameless ingratitude
See me as a white flag?

1981

Manuscript page from the Medieval Uyghur Buddhist Drama *Maitrisimit*,
written by Pïrtanrakshit Karmawazik, composed in 767 CE. Unearthed in Qumul, Uyghurstan in 1959.

# Three Poetry Fragments Unearthed at Turpan Bezeklik

Turpan settlement was once a strategic town on the Silk Road noted for its Buddhist culture during the medieval period, from the eighth to the eleventh centuries. Turpan is also the name given to the Turpan Basin, located northeast of the larger Tarim Basin. During medieval times, Turpan was the capital city of the Idïqut Uyghur Empire and a center of Uyghur culture. The territory of this kingdom varied over time, but the city and its immediate environs remained the political and cultural center of Uyghurstan throughout the fifteenth century. The remarkable Bezeklik Buddhist caves, about forty-six kilometers northeast of present-day Turpan, are evidence of the area's importance as a religious center. There are eighty-four grottoes carved into cliffs above a river that flows through a deep gorge.

Since 1975, Dolkun Kamberi has been involved in archeological field work in the Turpan Basin—a rich archeological site where extreme aridity has preserved many important artifacts that include naturally mummified human remains, artwork in bronze and gold, textiles, and petroglyphs. Numerous medieval Uyghur documents that chart both religious practice and economic development in the region have also been discovered. Fragments of Manichean stories and poems, Buddhist sutras, sutra colophons, and dedicatory odes have been found, along with evidence of socioeconomic development, including fragments of contracts, receipts for loans, official orders, and government documents. Many of the written documents are so well preserved that even today they remain clear and easy to decipher. The majority of the manuscripts unearthed from Bezeklik were written in the ancient Uyghur language. The medieval Uyghur civilization is reflected in their Buddhist literature, which remains one of their most important legacies. The three unearthed fragments selected here as examples were discovered in Turpan in the early 1980s.

Ülgüsüz Kalplartin Berüki Awan-lar Tïltaghlar,
Igid Sakinch Erser Kaltï Yawalagh Yaghi Tek Erür,
Az Amranmak Köngül Erser, Aghulugh Yïlangha Ohshayur,
Birok Kusush-te Turup Küsüshsüz Bulghalï Usar
Niz-wani-ta Turup Niz-wanika Yoklunmasar,
Yirtinchü Üze Tayansar Kikir-siz arigh Orunka,
Timin Ok Tanuklaghalï Uyur Nom Khaningge Tozin.

From the beginning of time, desire and vanity
have existed together, intertwined, one enemy.
A bitter, loveless heart is a poisonous snake.
But if one can live in an avaricious world free of greed,
in a discordant society uninfected by discord,
standing firmly on the earth, one will reach the unblemished
pure land and in an instant realize the body of a moral king.

FRAGMENT 1: 80 T.B. 1, 598

Bu Anchulayu Kalmish-la-ga Yiti Ardini-ila Tapinsar,
Ud'insar ol Buyan Edgü Kilinchi-ning Ülgisin Tegin;
Ulgulagali Sanaghali Bolghay, Amita Ayusi Sudur-qa;
Tapinmish Udunmish ol Ulgulagali Sanaghali Bolmas.

One who worships Buddha embraces the seven treasures:
Their merits and good deeds will be measurable.
But one who worships and respects this Sutra:
Their merits and good deeds will be immeasurable.

FRAGMENT 2: 80 T.B. I, 596-1

Özung-ning Ögrenmish Yandirlarta,
Ögline Edgü-Kime Busugh Silikil,
Ong-me Negu-kim Yangilarita,
Oslunch-singe Tegi Anchulayu Ol.
Umukluk Közüm Birle Okup Sanga Idim.

What knowledge you seek, learn your own way
Think more, grow in self-awareness, do not boast
Of that which you engage in, be vigilant and steady
That is how you will shine bright above others

I read this with hopeful eyes and send it to you

FRAGMENT 3: 80 T.B. 1, 522

# To Wake Up

Abduhalik Uyghur

Abduhalik Uyghur (1901-1933) was born into an intellectual family in the Turpan Prefecture of the Uyghur Autonomous Region in 1901. When he was twenty, Abduhalik traveled with his father to China, Russia, and Finland, as he wanted to observe different international cultural and political systems. After he returned, he began to write an overtly political poetry directed to the Uyghur people.

In 1932, he organized the Revolution Central Committee of Turpan to develop cultural and political activities. Not long after this he was arrested by the local Chinese warlord, Sheng Shicai, and sentenced to death. He was only thirty-two. Abduhalik's first poetry collection was published in the 1980s, fifty years after his death. His poem "To Wake Up" is famous in Uyghurstan.

# ئويغان !

ھەي، پېقىر ئۇيغۇر، ئويغان، ئۇيقۇڭ يېتەر،
سەندە مال يوق، ئەمدى كەتسە جان كېتەر.
بۇ ئۆلۈمدىن ئۆزۈڭنى قۇتقازمىساڭ،
ئاھ، سېنىڭ ھالىڭ خەتەر، ھالىڭ خەتەر.

قوپ! دېدىم، بېشىڭنى كۆتەر، ئۇيقۇڭنى ئاچ،
رەقىبىڭ بېشىنى كەس، قېنىنى چاچ.
كۆز ئېچىپ ئەتراپقا ئوبدان باقمىساڭ،
ئۆلسەن ئارماندا، بىر كۈن يوق ئىلاج.

ھېلىمۇ جانسىزغا ئوخشايدۇ تېنىڭ،
شۇڭا يوقمۇ ئانچە ئۆلۈمدىن غېمىڭ.
قىچقىرسام قىمىرلىمايلا ياتسەن،
ئويغانماي ئۆلمەكچىمۇ سەن شۇ پېتىڭ.

# To Wake Up

Ay! Uyghurs, my people, wake up, you have slept enough,
Nothing left to lose but precious life.
If you want to save yourselves from extinction,
Ah! Wake up! Our life is threatened, the situation is worsening.

Stand, I say, raise your head, and wake up,
It is time to raze the enemy, I call, be brave, fight, shed blood.
If you do not open your eyes and look carefully around you,
You will die with regret. No choice but to wake up.

Is there no difference, even now, between you and the dead?
Is this why you are still unmoved, as death quickly approaches?
Please, act now, join the call, awake from your deep sleep.
Or would you rather die sleeping? To never wake?

كۆزۈڭنى يوغان ئېچىپ ئەتراپقا باق،
ئوز ئىستىقبالىڭ ھەققىدە ئويلان ئۇزاق.
كەتسە قولدىن بۇ غېنىمەت، پۇرسەت،
كېلىچەك ئىشىڭ چاتاق، ئىشىڭ چاتاق.

ئېچىنار كۆڭلۈم ساڭا، ھەي ئۇيغۇرۇم،
سەبدىشىم، قېرىندىشىم، بىر تۇغقۇنۇم.
كۆيۈنۈپ ھالىڭغا ئويغاتسام سېنى،
ئاڭلىمايسەن زادى، نېمە بولغۇنۇڭ.

كېلىدۇ بىر كۈن پۇشايمان قىلسەن،
تەكتىگە گەپنىڭ شۇ چاغدا يېتىسەن.
""خەپ دېسەڭ شۇ چاغدا ئۈلگۈرمەي قالۇر،
شۇندا، ئۇيغۇر، سۆزىگە تەن بېرىسەن.

Open your eyes; be strong and unwavering, face the real
In thinking of your fate and the future of the Uyghurs.
If our nation loses this rare and precious chance,
Uyghurs will suffer, our lives will be misery.

My heart is bleeding, ay, my fellow Uyghurs,
My friends, my brothers and sisters, my family.
With my injured heart, with love, I try to wake you.
What is happening? Why don't you listen and rise up?

When that day comes, how sorry Uyghurs will be,
Then, you will understand the meaning of my call.
It will be too late for regret, too late to wake,
Only then, Uyghurs, my people, will you remember me.

1921

# Quatrains from the *Diwan Lughat al-Turk*

Mahmud al-Kashgari

The following poems from Mahmud al-Kashgari's Dictionary of the Turk Languages (*Diwan Lughat al-Turk*, or *Türki Tillar Divani,* or *Divan Lughatit Türk*), written in 1074 CE, give the reader some sense of the long tradition and history of Uyghur folk poetry that stretched back further than even Mahmud al-Kashgari's times.

The folk poetry and songs of Uyghurs very often consist of rhymed quatrains. There are thousands of them in Kashgari's *Divan*, in the medieval Turpan texts, and from other manuscripts. The few we include here give some insight into Uyghur hospitality, folk philosophy, festival celebrations, and general life-ways. The idea of how to entertain people in a friendly manner is a wonderful part of a theatrical social life that can be traced back nearly two thousand years.

# On Guests

Körklüg tonugh özängä
Tatlïgh ashïgh adïngha
Tutghïl qonuq aghïrlïgh
Yadsun qowïng bodunqa

Kälsär uma tüshürgil
Tïnsïn anïng aruqluq
Arpa saman yaghutghïl
Bulsïn atï yaruqluq

Dress yourself in a beautiful robe
Offer delicious food to your guest
Treat your visitor with respect
And your good name will spread

When a guest arrives, help him dismount
Make him feel at home and at ease
Mix barley and hay for his horse
And brush its coat to sleekness

# On Festivals

Ottuz ichip qïqïralïm
Yoqar qopup säkrälim
Arslanlayu kökrälim
Qachtï saqïnch säwnälim

✤

Yigitlärig ishlätü
Yighach yimish ïrghatu
Qulan kiyik awlatu
bädräm qïlïp awnalïm

Let us drink thirty glasses and sing
Then let us stand up and dance
To leap as a lion, roll and roar,
With cheers, chase sadness away

Let the young ones do the work
Shake fruit from the tree
Hunt wild horses and deer
For the festival, while we drink

# On Knowledge

Yusuf Hajib Balasaghuni and Ahmad Yuknaki

Education received the highest priority in medieval Uyghur society. Because they emphasized the value of acquiring knowledge and respecting scholars, medieval Uyghurstan became one of the strongest, most cultured countries in Asia at that time.

In Uyghur literature, the *Kutadgu Bilig* (Knowledge Leads to Happiness) by Yusuf Hajib Balasaghuni (c. 1019 – 1085) is one of the most important medieval sources of Uyghur culture. Hajib was born in the city of Balasaghun, the capital of the Karakhanid Empire, and later moved to Kashgar, where he completed this work. He presented it to the ruler of the Khanate and was granted the status of advisor to the Khan. Hajib believed that the world was composed of earth, water, gas, and fire, calling them the four fundamental elements that are constantly contradictory yet united, always in motion and renewing themselves. He believed that the universe, seven planets, twelve signs of the zodiac, and everything in the human world were inseparable from these four elements, their contradictory and harmonious state. A perfect society meant a harmonious society, and "knowledge brings social happiness." Besides the *Kutadgu Bilig*, Ahmad Yuknaki's *Atabet'ul Haqayiq* (The Gate of Truth, c. 12th century) is another important medieval source of poetry that celebrates the importance of knowledge and education. Below are five quatrains from these various medieval texts.

# On Knowledge

yaghiz yär qatïndaqï altun tash ol
qalï chïqsa bäglär bashïnda tush ol
biliklig chïqarmasa bilkin tilin
yarutmaz anïng bilki yatsa yilin

(Y. B.)

✤

bilig biling ya bägim
bilig sanga äsh bolur
bilig bilgän ol ärgä
bir kün däwlät tush bolur

(A.Y.)

✤

biliglig är biligä
tash qursansa qash bolur

# On Knowledge

Gold is only ore beneath russet earth
Unearthed becomes the ornament of a crown
If a scholar doesn't impart his knowledge
His wisdom, hidden for years, sheds no light

(Y. B.)

✤

To learn knowledge, yah my chieftain,
Knowledge that will always dwell in you
Knowledge that when understood
Will one day the land belong to

(A.Y.)

✤

If a learned man puts a stone in his belt,
the stone will turn to jade.

biligsizning yanïgha
altun qoysa tash bolur

(A.Y.)

✤

Yoq ärsär azunda bu ʻalim bögü
tikip önmägäy ärdi yärdä yägü
olar ʻilmi boldï bodunqa yula
yarusa yula tünlä azmaz yola

(Y. B.)

✤

bilig bildi boldï ärän bälgülüg
biligsiz tiriklä yitük körgülüg
biliglig är öldi atï ölmädi
biligsiz tirig ärkän atï ölüg

(A.Y.)

If an ignorant man carries gold with him,
the gold will turn to stone.

(A.Y.)

✤

If there are no scholars, no wise ones,
even grain will not grow from tilled land.
Their knowledge is a light for us humans,
if bright enough, will dispel the darkness.

(Y. B.)

✤

The knowledgeable are visible among us
The ignorant, even alive, are invisible
The knowledgeable die but live on in name
The ignorant alive are but dead names

(A.Y.)

# Motherland Shines My Heart

Dilber Keyim Kizi

Dilber Keyim Kizi was born in Kashgar in 1958. She graduated from Kashgar Teacher's College in 1975, and then worked as an editor for a literary magazine. She is a member of the Uyghur Regional Writers Association.

After publishing her first poem, "If I Become a Drop of Dew," in 1980, she gradually became a well-known woman poet among the Uyghurs. Her first poetry collection, *Dew*, was published in 1984, and she continues to publish poems and short stories. "Motherland Shines My Heart" was selected as her representative poem for the Uyghur Autonomous Region's thirty-year anniversary poetry anthology, *Joyful Celebration.*

# ۋەتەندىن نۇر ئىمىپ قەلبىم...

1

يېتەر مەن ئارزۇ-ئارمانغا ۋەتەننى ئىپتىخار ئەيلەپ،
گۈزەل جەننەت قۇچاغىدا يورۇشنى ئىختىيار ئەيلەپ.

بولۇپمەن ئىشقىدا بۇلبۇل چىمەنلەر ئىچرە سايرايمەن،
جاراڭلىق ناخشا توۋلايمەن يۈرەك رىشتىمنى تار ئەيلەپ.

كۆزۈم قارچۇغىدەك ئاسراپ ئۇنىڭ ھەر تال گىياسىنى،
قىلىپ تۇپراغىنى سۈرمە، گۈلىنى تىل - تۇمار ئەيلەپ.

ئاقار مېھرىم ياساپ ئۆركەش ۋەتەنگە ھەمدە خەلقىمگە،
ئۆمۈرۋايەت قىلىپ خىزمەت ئۆتۈشنى چىن - شۇئار ئەيلەپ.

ئەگەر يانسام ۋاپا قىلماي، ئۆزەمنىڭ ئەھدۇ - لەۋزىمدىن،
بولايكى مەن جۇدا جاندىن، قارا ساچىمنى دار ئەيلەپ.

# Motherland Shines My Heart

1

To be proud of my country is my hope, my desire, to walk
freely in the beauty of its heavenly cradle, my wanting.

I am my motherland's crazed lover; I sing like a nightingale
in the garden, pluck the veins of my heart like strings

to play my sonorous praise-song. I protect each plant of my country
as I would my own eyes; I use her soil as cream, her flowers

as symbols of fortune. My sweat flows in waves for my beloved
country, my people, my life I vow to devote to our freedom.

I would rather hang myself with my long braided black hair
than betray my people with empty promises.

غۇبارسىز پاك يۈرەك ـ قەلبى ۋەتەندىن نۇر ئېمىپ مەڭگۈ
سۆيەر دىلبەر ۋۇجۇدىدىن ۋەتەننى مەڭگۈ يار ئەيلەپ.

2

ۋەتەن ئىشقىدا سەن بولغىن ۋاپا پەرۋانىسى، دىلبەر،
يېرىپ بۈركۈت كەبى كۆكنى زامان مەردانىسى، دىلبەر.

ئېلىپ بارسا سابا ياڭراق كۈيۈك ـ ناخشاڭنى گۈلباققا،
كۆڭۈلنى مەھلىيا قىلسۇن سۆزۈڭ دۇردانىسى، دىلبەر.

ئۈرۈنسا گەر ھەسەتخورلار گۈلۈڭنى چەيلىمەككە قەست،
ئۇلارغا ئوق بولۇپ تەگسۇن كۆزۈڭ پەيكانىسى، دىلبەر.

تۆكۈپ ساپ قان بىلەن تەرنى گۈلۈڭنى پەرۋىرش ئەيلە،
بېغىڭ بولسۇن شۇ خەلقىڭنىڭ سەيىر ئاستانىسى، دىلبەر.

3

ھەم جاپالىق ھەم شەرەپلىك تاللىغان مەنزىل يولۇم،
ئارزۇيۇم شۇ تالمىسۇن ھەرگىز، قەلەم تۇتقان قولۇم.

The light of the motherland shines, purifies my bewildered
heart; my soul is bound to her as a lover forever.

2

As eagles soar across the open blue sky, I follow the traces
of my ancestral heroes; fireflies circle the light, how could I leave

this land unguarded. My heart fills with love, my words turn to pearls,
I bring my song to the flowering garden at dawn.

If profit-mad men deceive you and tread on your flowers,
let my eyelashes become spears to pierce the intruders.

With willing blood, sweat, shed to nourish your flowers,
the garden can become a replenishing–place for the people.

3

This is the impossible, glorious path I have chosen;
if only my pen would not dry, my hand not tire.

چۈنكى ۋىجدان چىللىدى :چۈش جەڭگە دەپ پەرمان قىلىپ،
شۇ خىتاپ بىرلە ئېتىلدى ئالغا ئىلھام دۇلدۇلۇم.

دوستلىرىمغا جۆر بولۇپ سايراي ئىجات گۈل باغىدا،
خۇشپۇراق چاچسۇن ھەمىشە لالە، رەيھان، سۇمبۇلۇم.

ۋەتىنىم، خەلقىم ئۈچۈن تۆككەن تېرىم مەھسۇلىدىن،
ئارزۇيۇم شۇدۇر ئېچىلسا نەۋ باھارىمدا گۈلۈم.

شۇ ئەقىدەمدىن ئېچىلغان گۈلنى قىسسا، دوستلىرىم،
نىمە ئارمان بىر ئۆمۈر شات سايرىسا شوخ بۇلبۇلۇم.

For it is my conscience that summons my mind to words,
a summoning of knowledge that bounds swiftly forward.

I have joined hands with my friends in palaces, in gardens,
sent forth the fragrance of blossoming flowers.

My sweat for my beloved country, my people, is what
makes this flower-bloom flourish in dawn spring.

If my friends carry the blossoms of my will and my care,
regrets disappear, as the nightingale sings wild forever.

FEBRUARY 1982

# Editors

**Natasha Wimmer** is the translator of Roberto Bolaño's *The Savage Detectives* (Farrar Straus & Giroux, 2007) and *2666* (2009). She has also translated novels and nonfiction by Mario Vargas Llosa, Rodrigo Fresán, Laura Restrepo, and Gabriel Zaid, among others. She is a regular contributor to *The Nation*, and has written for the *New York Times*, the *Believer*, and the *American Scholar*.

**Jeffrey Yang** is a poet, translator, and editor at New Directions Publishing. He is the author of the poetry books *An Aquarium* and the forthcoming *Vanishing-Line* (Fall 2011), both with Graywolf Press. He has translated Su Shi's *East Slope* (Ugly Duckling Presse) and a collection of classical Chinese poems called *Rhythm 226*. An anthology of nature poems from New Directions he edited will be published in Spring 2011.

# Contributors

**Aftab Ahmad** earned his PhD in Urdu literature from Jawaharlal Nehru University in New Delhi. After serving as the Director of the American Institute of Urdu Studies Program in Lucknow for five years, he began teaching as an Urdu lecturer at the University of California, Berkeley in 2006.

**Kurt Beals** is a PhD student in German at the University of California, Berkeley, focusing on modern German literature, translation, and critical theory. His translations of authors including Ernst Jandl and Alexander Kluge have appeared in publications including *n+1* and *Dimension2*. His translation of Anja Utler's *engulf—enkindle* is forthcoming from Burning Deck Press.

**Rebecca Bella** is a poet, playwright, and translator. She translates from Russian and Spanish and produced the film "Poets Address: St. Petersburg" (2008). Her poetry has appeared in *236*, *Poets 11*, and *Left Curve*. Her translations have been published in *A Public Space*, the *Saint Petersburg Review*, and by Ugly Duckling Presse, and she participated in the San Francisco International Poetry Festival of 2009 with Alexander Skidan. Her play "TERRORiSTKA" was produced in Berkeley, California in 2010.

**Gabrielle Civil** is a black woman poet, conceptual and performance artist, originally from Detroit, Michigan. She is an Associate Professor of English, Women's Studies, and Critical Studies of Race & Ethnicity at St. Catherine University in St. Paul, Minnesota. The aim of all her work is to open up space.

**Heather Cleary Wolfgang**'s translations into English of the poetry, prose, and literary criticism of Oliverio Girondo, Sergio Chejfec and Mariano Siskind have been published in journals such as the *Literary Review*, *New York Tyrant* and *Habitus*, and in the anthology *Reading Otherwise: The Ethics of Latin American Literary Criticism* (Palgrave Macmillan, 2007). She received a PEN Translation Fund grant for her work with the poetry of Oliverio Girondo in 2005 and is currently working toward a PhD in Columbia's department of Spanish and Portuguese.

**Elliott Colla** teaches Arabic literature and literary translation at Georgetown University. He has translated works of Arabic fiction by Ibrahim Aslan, Yahya al-Tahir 'Abdallah, Ghada 'Abdel Meneim, Rabai al-Madhoun, and is currently translating Ibrahim al-Koni's masterpiece, *al-Majus* (The Animists). He is also the author of *Conflicted Antiquities: Egyptology, Egyptomania, Egyptian Modernity* (Duke University Press, 2007), and numerous critical articles on Arab literature, film, and culture.

**Jennifer Croft** holds an MFA in Literary Translation from The University of Iowa and is now completing her PhD in Comparative Literary Studies at Northwestern University. She also translates from Spanish, and currently lives in Paris.

**Lydia Davis**—MacArthur "genius," National Book Award finalist, chevalier of the Order of Arts and Letters—won the 2003 French-American Foundation Translation Prize for her translation of Marcel Proust's *Swann's Way*. Her *Collected Stories* was one of the most acclaimed books of 2009. Davis lives near Albany, New York.

**Peter France** was born in Londonderry in 1935 and currently lives in Edinburgh, where he was a professor of French. He has published widely on French, Russian, and comparative literature, including the *Oxford Guide to Literature in English Translation* (Oxford University Press, 2001), and has translated many books of French prose and Russian poetry.

**Dr. Dolkun Kamberi,** the founding Director of Radio Free Asia Uyghur Service since 1998, earned his MPhil and PhD degrees from Columbia University, and completed his post-doctoral research at the University of Pennsylvania. He is an internationally recognized scholar and authority on the ancient Silk Road civilization and Sino-Turkic languages. Dr. Kamberi's career has spanned work as a field-archeologist, university professor, linguist, translator, and Uyghur media specialist. He has been invited to speak at many universities throughout the U.S. and at international conferences around the world, talking on subjects related to Central Asian political, cultural, historical, linguistic, archeological, and human rights issues. His articles on Silk-Road civilization have been published extensively in many languages.

**Sarah Rebecca Kersley** was born and raised in Britain and holds an MA in Hispanic Studies from the University of Glasgow. She is a freelance translator specializing in translation for academic journals, particularly in the area of Brazilian literature. In 2005, she moved to Northeast Brazil, where she founded Urso de Óculos, the only bookshop in her adopted hometown.

**Eddin Khoo** is a poet, writer, translator and journalist. He serves as Founder-Director of the cultural organization *Pusaka*.

**Lucas Klein** is the editor of www.CipherJournal.com. His translations, essays, and poems have appeared at *Jacket, Drunken Boat, Mānoa*, and *Big Bridge*, and he regularly reviews books for *Rain Taxi* and other venues. A co-editor of *The Chinese Written Character as a Medium for Poetry: A Critical Edition*, by Ernest Fenollosa and

Ezra Pound (Fordham, 2008), he will be teaching translation at City University of Hong Kong following his PhD in Chinese from Yale.

**Suzanne Jill Levine** is currently general editor of Penguin Classics' five-volume 2010 series of the prose and poetry of Jorge Luis Borges. An eminent translator as well as scholar of Latin American literature and Translation Studies, her books include *Manuel Puig and the Spider Woman: His Life and Fictions* (Farrar Straus & Giroux, 2001) and *The Subversive Scribe: Translating Latin American Fiction*, reissued by Dalkey Archive Press (2009).

**Rick London**'s publications include *Dreaming Close By* (O Books, 1986), *Abjections: A Suite* (O Books, 1988), and *The Materialist* (Doorjamb Press, 2008). He is co-translator (with Omnia Amin) of works in Arabic by Mahmoud Darwish, Nawal El Saadawi, and Ibrahim Nasrallah. He lives and works in San Francisco.

**Fayre Makeig** lives in New York, where she is a student in Columbia University's MFA program. Her poems have appeared in the *Western Humanities Review*. In 2009, she won a PEN translation fund grant for the selected free verse of H. E. Sayeh.

**Arvind Krishna Mehrotra** is the author of four books of poems, the most recent of which is *The Transfiguring Places* (Sangam Books, 1998). His translations of Kabir will be published by New York Review Books Classics in 2011.

**Susanna Nied**'s award-winning translations of Inger Christensen's *alphabet*, *Butterfly Valley: A Requiem*, and *it* were published by New Directions in 2000, 2003, and 2006. Her translations of Christensen's *Light*, *Grass*, and *Letter in April*, awarded the 2009 John Frederick Nims Poetry Prize for Translation, are forthcoming from New Directions.

**Ahmatjan Osman** was born in 1964 in Urumqi,

Uyghurstan. His first collection of poems was published in Uyghur in 1982. That year he also received a scholarship to study Arabic literature in Damascus, Syria. In 2004, he was deported from Syria under pressure from the Chinese government, and he settled in Canada as a political refugee. Osman has published eight volumes of poetry, six written in Arabic, and two in Uyghur.

**Jessica Ernst Powell** holds an MA in Latin American Studies from Stanford University and a PhD in Hispanic Languages and Literatures from the University of California, Santa Barbara. She has published numerous translations of a wide variety of Latin American authors, including Jorge Luis Borges, César Vallejo, Edgardo Rivera Martínez, María Moreno, Edmundo Paz-Soldán, Liliana Heer, Alan Pauls, and Anna Lidia Vega Serova, as well as a play, *Persistence Until Death*, by the Spanish Golden Age playwright Lope de Vega.

**Matt Reeck** is a writer living in Brooklyn. *Midwinter*, his third chapbook of poetry, was released in January 2010, by Fact-Simile Press; *My Dictionary*, his fourth, is forthcoming from Dirty Swan Projects. He has translated work from the Urdu of Saadat Hasan Manto, Premchand, and Patras Bukhari.

**Raphael Rubinstein** has published several collections of poetry and art criticism. He is also the translator of Marcel Cohen's *In Search of a Lost Ladino* (Ibis Editions, 2006). He is based in New York City and is Professor of Critical Studies at the University of Houston School of Art.

**Marian Schwartz** translates Russian fiction and nonfiction and is the principal English translator of the works of Nina Berberova. Her translation of Olga Slavnikova's novel *2017*, which won the Russian Booker Prize, was published by Overlook Press in 2010. Schwartz is a past president of the American Literary Translators Association.

**Eric Selland** is a poet and translator living on the San Francisco peninsula. His translations of modernist and contemporary Japanese poets have appeared in a variety of journals and anthologies. He has also published articles on Japanese modernist poetry and translation theory. He is the author of *The Condition of Music* (Sink Press, 2000), *Inventions* (Seeing Eye Books, 2007), and an essay in *The Poem Behind the Poem: Translating Asian Poetry* (Copper Canyon Press, 2004). Eric is currently editing an anthology of 20th century Japanese modernist and avant -garde poetry.

**Katherine Silver** has translated the works of many Spanish and Latin American authors, including Antonio Skármeta, José Emilio Pacheco, Elena Poniatowska, Martín Adán (for which she received a NEA grant), Pedro Lemebel, and Jorge Franco. For her translation of Horacio Castellanos Moya's *Senselessness* (New Directions, 2008), she received the 2008 NCBA Translation Award. She has translated plays, screenplays, and a wide assortment of academic and other nonfiction books. She also works as an editor and publishing consultant/manager, and lives in Berkeley, California.

**Joel Streicker**'s translations of stories by Ricardo Silva Romero, Luis Fayad, and Samanta Schweblin have or are scheduled to appear in *Words without Borders, The Bitter Oleander*, and *Subtropics*. His book reviews have appeared in *The Forward* and other publications. Streicker holds a PhD in anthropology from Stanford University.

**Clare Sullivan**, an Associate Professor of Spanish at the University of Louisville, specializes in contemporary

Latin American poetry. She published a translation of Argentine Alicia Kozameh's *250 Saltos, uno inmortal* in 2007 and Mexican Cecilia Urbina's *Un martes como hoy* in 2008, both with Wings Press.

**Teng Qian Xi** is from Singapore and graduated from Columbia University. Her poems have appeared in *Language for a New Century* (W. W. Norton, 2008), the London Underground's *Poems on the Underground*, *Quarterly Literary Review Singapore*, and elsewhere. Her first collection, *They hear salt crystallising*, was published by firstfruits publications in 2010.

**Sarah Valentine** is a poet and translator. She received a PhD in Russian Literature from Princeton University and recently completed a postdoctoral fellowship at the University of California, Los Angeles. She has two books on Gennady Aygi, a monograph and a volume of poetry translations, forthcoming in 2011. She lives in Los Angeles with her husband.

**Henry Whittlesey** is a writer and translator of Russian and German literature. His translations, essays and papers have appeared in *New Madrid*, *Arch Literary Journal*, *Transfer Review*, *Comparative Literature and Culture*, and elsewhere. He is currently composing a transposition based on the intersecting of *Dead Souls* by Gogol and *Persuasion* by Austen. He lives in New York.

# Index

by Author

# Index

by Title

# Index

by Language

# A Note on the Translations

Original texts appear across from their translations. Where feasible, the entire original text is provided for each of the translations; however, space concerns have prevented the inclusion of more than the first page of prose pieces. Excerpts are marked by spaced ellipses. Copyright permission remains the responsibility of the contributors.

In order to express regional differences in language usage, we make every attempt to locate the authors within the literary tradition of a particular country or geographical region. The region is indicated in parentheses following the language on each title page.

# Acknowledgments

Pp. 16-24 excerpted from *Madame Bovary* by Gustave Flaubert. Reprinted by arrangement with Viking Penguin, a member of Penguin Group (USA) Inc. Translation copyright © 2010 by Lydia Davis.

Pp. 138-140 "A Few Notes on Poetry" excerpted from *Poems by Gennady Aygi.* Translation copyright © 2010 by Sarah Valentine. Used by permission of Wave Books.

Pp. 156-162 "for daphne: lamented" excerpted from *münden – entzüngeln* by Anja Utler. Copyright © 2004 by Edition Korrespondenzen, Franz Hammerbacher, Vienna. Translation copyright © 2010 by Kurt Beals. Used by permission of Burning Deck Press.

Pp. 238-240 "Translation is a Testing Ground" by Roberto Bolaño. Copyright © 2004 by The Heirs of Roberto Bolaño. Translation copyright © 2010 by Natasha Wimmer. Used permission of New Directions Publishing Corporation. All rights reserved.

The editors would like to thank Keith Ekiss, Annie Janusch, and Shimon Tanaka for their work on this edition.

# About TWO LINES

For seventeen years, TWO LINES has published translations of essential international voices unavailable anywhere else. Every edition showcases diverse new writing alongside the world's most celebrated authors, and presents exclusive insight from the translators into the creative art of translation. The annual anthology TWO LINES: World Writing in Translation and the World Library series are a testament to the expanse of voices in the world, and shows readers how universal the themes and struggles of humanity are.

TWO LINES is a program of the Center for the Art of Translation, a non-profit organization that promotes cultural dialogue, international literature, and translation through publishing, teaching, and public events. In addition to the TWO LINES publications, the Center makes global voices and great literature accessible to individuals and communities through the Poetry Inside Out educational program and Lit&Lunch, the only reading series spotlighting translation.

### JOIN US

As a non-profit publisher, TWO LINES relies on readers and writers like you to help support our efforts to share the importance of translation as a vital bridge between languages and people. Please consider making a donation to the Center. Find out more or make a pledge at www.catranslation.org

# Oh, Night

Ahmatjan Osman | Translated by Ahmatjan Osman and Jeffrey Yang from Arabic (Uyghurstan)

What passed was your night
oh, night, what passed was upcoming.
This is my ancient ode
falling as a star from your infinite heights;
this is my rebellious soul
climbing from your depths like a blind snake.

What passed was your shade
oh, night, what passed was upcoming.
I walk tripping my way across your steps
dawn . . .
after dawn . . .
the dust-covered copper bells
of my young dream dies, as I
hold the breasts of the sun.

What passed was your sun
oh, night, what passed was upcoming.
I am here, her sad lover, in your eternity,
I rise
from my death like a god
and, silently, sing her just descent,
while she hides in twilight delight
as if in darkness-enclosing sin.

What passed was your night
oh, night, what passed was upcoming.
Where I am still, and will stay,
your passing mask, same as the falling star,
your transient one, same as the twilight . . .